NOT WHO
YOU THINK

NOT WHO YOU THINK

A NOVEL

ARBOR SLOANE

NEW YORK

Books should be disposed of and recycled according to local requirements. All paper materials used are FSC compliant.

This is a work of fiction. All of the names, characters, organizations, places and events portrayed in this novel are either products of the author's imagination or are used fictitiously. Any resemblance to real or actual events, locales, or persons, living or dead, is entirely coincidental.

Copyright © 2025 by Arbor Sloane

All rights reserved.

Published in the United States by Crooked Lane Books, an imprint of The Quick Brown Fox & Company LLC.

Crooked Lane Books and its logo are trademarks of The Quick Brown Fox & Company LLC.

Library of Congress Catalog-in-Publication data available upon request.

ISBN (hardcover): 979-8-89242-217-8
ISBN (paperback): 979-8-89242-277-2
ISBN (ebook): 979-8-89242-218-5

Cover design by Danna Steele

Printed in the United States.

www.crookedlanebooks.com

Crooked Lane Books
34 West 27th St., 10th Floor
New York, NY 10001

First Edition: August 2025

The authorized representative in the EU for product safety and compliance is eucomply OÜ Pärnu mnt 139b-14, 11317 Tallinn, Estonia, hello@eucompliancepartner.com, +33757690241

10 9 8 7 6 5 4 3 2 1

For my Father

CHAPTER

1

The Kidnapper

Iowa City, 2024

THE FALLING SNOW makes it difficult to see much in the parking lot of the coffee shop, Freshly Ground, where I sit behind the wheel, barely breathing, knowing that *she* is sitting only about a hundred feet away. I can't see her inside, but I can feel her there.

Renee relayed the girl's coordinates earlier, and she is never wrong when it comes to these things. I read her message again as I wait, nodding along to "Voodoo" by Godsmack on my truck's stereo. Don't fuck this up, she texted me about twenty minutes ago. This is your chance. It's true. Every crime leading up to this has been preparing me for this moment. I tap my fingers against my thigh as I mentally make sure everything is in order. Piled on the passenger seat, I have a roll of duct tape, a syringe loaded with a hefty dose of ketamine, and my insurance policy, a Colt Mustang that has been with me through thick and thin.

I thumb open my phone and go through the photos I saved from the girl's Instagram, which she leaves wide open even though she should know better, given her mother's occupation. In fact, she looks just like her mother, with long auburn hair, wide-set eyes, and a Cupid's-bow mouth that quirks up into a half smile when she's posing for a selfie. Innocent, like something off one of those Disney shows. Teenagers. It's like they don't know people like me exist. But this girl, she should realize the dangers inherent with posting pictures of herself for just anyone to see. Lucky for me, she obviously doesn't.

In one photo, she is sitting in a restaurant booth with a gangly kid about her age—maybe sixteen—wearing a blue Vans t-shirt. His arm is slung around her neck. Two red coffee mugs sit steaming on the table in front of them. I wonder if the picture was taken at this coffee shop. Maybe he's sitting inside with her right now. I imagine what I'll do if he comes outside with her. It'll put a wrench in things, but that's what the gun is for. I bet he's a coward. All I'll have to do is level it at him and tell him to lie down in the snow and count to a hundred and he'll do what I say. I bet there's no bravery in his eyes. He won't put up a fight when I take the girl. He won't dare.

My heart hammers beneath my jacket. I'm so sweaty, I think about taking it off but decide against it. I'll be getting out of the truck soon enough. I open the glove compartment and retrieve my copy of the book the girl's mother wrote. It's well worn from the million times I've read it over the years, with dog-eared pages and passages underlined in red. In a way, it's my guidebook. It's taught me everything I've needed to know since I started my dark journey.

The cover is all black and red, with an old-timey computer screen on the cover. On the monitor is the title, *Beyond the Glass*, which I can only imagine refers to the dangers of the Internet, the way Gerald Shapiro caught his victims, pretending to be different people online. I don't know if they called it catfishing back then, but that's what it was. The book details his life story, from when he was a kid just developing his methods, to the very end when he was caught.

I won't be caught.

Gerald was good, but not as good as me.

I flip to the back cover and stare at the picture of the girl's mother, Amelia Child. I wonder what she'd do if she knew I was about to steal away the most precious thing in her life. Closing my eyes, I imagine the way she'll collapse when she learns I've got her daughter in my basement. It will destroy her. The irony, the atrocities that she detailed in her book being exacted upon the one she loves most.

A noise brings me to my senses.

The ringing of a bell to announce the departure of a customer from the coffee shop. I shove the book back into my glove compartment and grab my gun, stuffing it into my pocket, and wait.

A girl rounds the corner, and my breath catches. Her dark hair blows across her face in the wind, but I recognize her red coat from her pictures on Instagram. She leans over her purse, searching for something. I pause for a second, waiting for the boyfriend to come out and accompany her, but a few seconds pass and I breathe out slowly.

She's alone.

Totally and completely alone.

After pulling my mask down over my face, I ease my door open, drift into the shadows, and creep toward her. She straightens up, keys in her hands, and heads for one of the cars parked in the corner. Adrenaline blasts through my veins. I close the distance between us in four long strides, sneaking up behind her.

She must hear the snow crunch beneath my feet because she starts to turn around, but before she sees me, I sink the syringe of ketamine deep into her neck and press the plunger all the way down. She shrieks and then slumps into my arms. I drag her back to my truck and open the back door before pushing her inside. Her dark hair spills over her face, into her slightly open mouth, her arms falling helplessly at her sides. I reach past her and grab the duct tape, ripping a generous length off with my teeth and slapping it across her mouth before securing her wrists and ankles. She falls to the side, face hitting the cold seat, and I spread a blue flannel blanket over her, in case anyone should look inside my back window.

Just as I'm slamming the door closed, I hear the bell ring again. I jump back inside my truck, making sure my mask is in place. The engine roars to life, and I put the truck into drive, pulling out of the parking lot before I can see who has emerged from the coffee shop, before they can see me.

Within minutes, I'm on the interstate, my trophy in the back seat. Snow comes down on my windshield, my wipers barely able to keep up with the assault. No matter. All the better for me. There will be no tracks, no evidence. My temples throb with the blood pumping through me, and I pull off my mask, gulping in the cold air and letting out a scream of triumph.

CHAPTER

2

Beyond the Glass

(A. Child, 2019, pp. 1–2)

When people think of Gerald Shapiro, they think of the Catfish Killer, the man who created false profiles on the Internet to lure women to their deaths from beyond the glass of their computer monitors. The man who evolved along with social media, first using chat rooms in the early nineties, to MySpace in the early aughts, to Facebook and Instagram later on. The man who was convicted of the deaths of eighteen women. Here, I attempt to make sense of the violence wreaked upon our communities, to understand how a man like Gerald could do the things he did.

Gerald Shapiro wasn't always a monster, and perhaps that's the most frightening thing about him. When children are young, they are pure potential. Parents tell their kids they can be whatever they want. A doctor, a lawyer, the President of the United States. Nobody thinks their child is going to grow up to kidnap, rape, and murder young women. If that were the case, no one would ever procreate.

The question that many people ponder is whether someone is born a psychopath or develops the condition as a result of their environment. Dozens of interviews with Shapiro's parents and other relatives have resulted in a blurry picture of his childhood. Gerald was born in November of 1980. His father, Tom, worked in a meat-packing plant when he was young, and his mother Vera stayed at home to take care of him and his younger brother. They struggled with money, but most people thought the two seemed normal from the outside. That was before I scratched the surface and learned that the cracks of Gerald's foundation started from the very beginning.

When Gerald was born, Vera displayed signs of what is now known as postpartum depression, but there wasn't much known about the condition at the time. Her sister, Claire, said that Vera would rarely sleep, Gerald was always hungry, and Vera wasn't producing enough milk. He would wake her every forty-five minutes to feed, and she felt like a zombie most days.

The lack of sleep caused within Vera a sort of psychosis, and she'd sometimes wander outside and walk around the neighborhood, leaving Gerald alone, screaming. When Claire discovered this was happening, she moved in with the family for a time, helping to take care of the baby. This only enabled Tom to feel free to spend more time at the bars with his buddies, while Vera struggled with pumping enough to satisfy Gerald.

When Gerald began sleeping for longer periods of time, allowing Vera to get some rest, Claire moved out but kept a close eye on the family, not trusting Tom when he was drunk. He was known to get violent when he had a few beers under his belt, and more than once, Vera called Claire, crying that Tom had hit her. Despite Claire's insistence that Vera leave Tom, she stayed with him. Love can be a vicious thing sometimes. She was caught up in the cycle of abuse—the chaos, the apologies, the good times and the bad.

Also, Tom was the sole provider for the family. Vera and her boys would never make it on their own. She had to think about more than herself. She had to think about her sons.

CHAPTER 3

Amelia

Iowa City, 2024

BEING A PARENT is a blessing. I tell myself this as I pick up dirty laundry from Gabby's bedroom floor. The room is massive compared to my bedroom growing up, so there's twice as much room for her to spread out her mess. There's a leaning tower of dirty t-shirts piled next to her already overflowing hamper. Jeans are crumpled wherever she shed them. Bras and underwear are scattered among her basketball gear and flute case and laptop. I gather all the dirty clothes I can and throw them into the laundry basket I've set upon her unmade bed.

When we moved in, Jack argued that no girl needed a room so big, but we had just received my advance on *Beyond the Glass* and I wanted to give her the very best—room to spread out and practice her hobbies, huge bookshelves to hold all the young adult romances she loves so much, and a private bathroom to decorate herself. Perhaps there's a little part of me that feels guilty for all the time I spent away on book tours and signings, but I genuinely wanted the best for her.

Sometimes I worry that I'm doing Gabby a disservice, raising her in this huge house and funding every little whim her heart desires. But then I feel guilty about divorcing Jack and I can't bring myself to not spoil her a little. Still, a sixteen-year-old girl should be responsible enough to do her own laundry.

Would it kill you to throw your dirty underwear into the hamper? I text her. Where are you, anyway?

She texts back with a pin showing the little coffee shop she and her boyfriend, Easton, like to go to after school. They're always out together, somewhere. It makes me a little nervous, her being out wandering around, given the disappearances in the past year, but Easton has impressed me with his responsibility, always getting her home on time and being totally respectful every time I've chatted with him.

I toss the phone onto the bed and reach under her covers to look for any discarded pajamas that need to be washed. My hand grazes something hard and unyielding. I pull back the covers, and that's when I see it. The book that both launched my career and paid for this house.

The red-and-black cover stares back at me mockingly. The 1990s computer emblazoned with the title, *Beyond the Glass*. A title my editor and I went back and forth on for ages. I flip it over and read the text on the back, describing

Geraldo Shapiro's life as a catfish, ensnaring the hearts of women all over the Midwest, only to lure them to their demise.

It's a book that made waves in the true crime community for exploring a new era of technological possibilities available to those with ill intent. It's a book that has earned me not only thousands of fans but also more than a few stalkers. In the beginning of my career, readers sent my publisher fawning letters and gifts. But, as the months went by and the book gained more notoriety, I started receiving creepier letters and even death threats from Shapiro's admirers. Now I stash everything in a box in my closet, unopened. Still, I get emails from all manner of reporters trying to secure an interview for their radio shows or podcasts.

I've tried to protect my daughter from the brunt of the media attention, but she still has kids at school who tease her about my fascination with the macabre. One kid even tried to get her expelled by sneaking a Swiss army knife into her backpack and saying Gabby was planning on attacking her teacher. It's been a rough ride, but she's turned out pretty well adjusted.

I suppose it was only a matter of time before she snuck the book under her covers to read with a flashlight. Honestly, I thought it would happen when she was much younger. I should be grateful that it's taken her this long to crack the book, but it doesn't make it any easier to know the evil she is being exposed to.

That I've exposed her to.

My mind goes back to the latest disappearance, Madison Dean, a girl about Gabby's age. Her laptop revealed that she'd been chatting with a guy she met on Instagram who kept liking her posts. They'd talked for a while, and she agreed to meet him in a park one day in October. A public place, she probably thought, somewhere safe surrounded by children and their harried mothers, a place she could trust. She didn't know that it would rain that day, keeping most people home.

The police found Madison's car parked there, and it wasn't until weeks later that her body was found in a ditch some towns over. She was wearing clothes her parents didn't recognize, and her face was overly made up, with heavy lipstick and smeared mascara. I couldn't help but think how this most recent crime resembled Gerald's and the way that he got women online to trust him, to meet up with him so he could dress them up and pose them the way he wanted them before disposing of their bodies. It's stories like these that keep me up at night.

I look back at the pin Gabby texted me, reassuring myself that she is safe and just where she's supposed to be.

Suddenly I am so tired. Being on pins and needles all of the time takes a toll on you. I lie back on Gabby's bed and decide to rest my eyes, just for a little while. I'm not sure how much time passes before I hear the front door open and close. I yawn and stretch. Gabby calls out my name, and I yell, "Up here!" She appears in the doorway a few seconds later.

"Mom?"

Seeing me in her room, she eyes me suspiciously. Her gaze falls upon the book I dropped back onto her bed. "What are you doing in my room?"

I gesture to the book lying on her comforter. "What are you doing with that book?"

She tucks her hair behind her ear and sits down on her daisy bedspread, a stark contrast to the gory cover of the book in her hands. I've got her there. I told her to not read it without telling me, that I wanted to be able to prepare her for the experience. She knows the world can be a cold and difficult place, but I'm not ready for her to comprehend the cruel and inhumane acts that some humans are capable of.

"I just wanted . . . to know."

Curiosity.

There's nothing simpler and nothing more dangerous.

She sinks onto the bed beside me.

I sigh and wrap my arms around her. "You could have asked me."

Holding her, I marvel at how much she's grown over the past few years. Had I really not noticed that she, somewhere along the way, had become a young woman? When she started insisting on choosing her own clothes at the mall? When she started driving? When she got a serious boyfriend? No, I saw it happening. I just didn't want it to. Which isn't fair to her.

"You've been worried about other stuff," she says, and a surge of guilt sweeps through me. It's true that, since Jack and I have split, I've been preoccupied with a number of things: untangling our finances, preparing a new book proposal for my editor, cleaning and maintaining this giant house that we bought during the "honeymoon" phase of my first book release. I never knew that it would become the albatross around my neck, endlessly taunting me for being so audacious to believe that I could live happily ever after.

"That's fair," I admit. "I wish you would have told me you wanted to read it. There are things I wanted to explain to you beforehand."

"Such as?"

"This book..." I begin, taking it from her hands.

I flip through it, landing on a few black-and-white photographs printed in the middle. Geraldo Shapiro's senior picture is on the left, an image of him in the nineties, wearing his blonde hair long and sporting a Pantera t-shirt. He was a handsome boy, but the knowledge of his extreme depravity turned him into a wolf for me. It is this picture that so many of his female admirers fell in love with. No one could look so angelic and be so evil. But he was.

"This book will change your view of the world. Reading about the things that Gerald Shapiro did will haunt you. You'll never think of people the same way again."

"Mom, I already know. He raped and murdered women. Have you seen what's on TV these days? It's nothing new to me."

"There are worse things. Very. Bad. Things," I warn her.

She stares back at me challengingly.

This is not the way I want to be raising her. I've never dictated what she read before. I'm on the committee against banned books in schools, for goodness' sake. It feels almost hypocritical to not stand behind what I wrote. After all, I tried to end the book with a glimmer of hope, the knowledge that Gerald Shapiro is behind bars now. The judge decided to give him the gift that he denied all those women, life. Two wrongs don't make a right. And that is the message I want to leave with her—that horrible things happen, but everything turns out alright in the end.

Good wins, not evil.

"You're old enough to decide what you want to read. But promise me that you'll come to me if it's too much for you."

She gives me a rueful smile.

"If you had it your way, I wouldn't read the book until I'm thirty."

I snap the book shut and meet her gaze. "If I had it my way, you'd never read it."

CHAPTER

4

Beyond the Glass

(A. Child, 2019, pp. 3–4)

CHILDREN ARE SUPPOSED to be innocent, with brains like a wad of brand-new Silly Putty, completely fresh until experiences imprint themselves into the clay. In the wake of his crimes, people have speculated ad nauseam on Gerald Shapiro's childhood.

Basically, what went wrong?

Because there is no refuting the fact that something seriously did.

The defining moment of his childhood came when he was five years old and his brother was two. During an interview, his mother described the evening as typical:

It was around six o'clock, after dinner. I'd already bathed Gerald and settled him down in bed with a Little Golden

Book. I had Noah in the bathtub and was washing his hair when the telephone rang. The water wasn't deep. I didn't think anything of it.

The call didn't last long. It was my sister calling to set up a dinner date. We chatted for a couple of minutes before settling on the following weekend. By the time I got off the phone, I heard Gerald crying. Not in bed, where I'd tucked him in, but from the bathroom. I rushed down the hall to see what was wrong, expecting to see that he'd had an accident and would need another bath. That happened sometimes. He drank too much water before bed and waited until the very last moment to head to the toilet.

But that's not what I found when I reached the bathroom.

Gerald was standing next to the bathtub. His hands were covering his eyes, and he was wailing his head off. It took me a moment to realize that Noah was still in the tub. His head was fully submerged and he wasn't moving. I pushed Gerald out of the way and scooped Noah into my arms. He wasn't breathing. I laid him on the bath mat and attempted to perform CPR, but it had been years since my training and I couldn't remember the steps.

Was it two short breaths and five chest compressions? I didn't know.

I screamed at Gerald to call 911, but he just stood there crying.

Noah still wasn't breathing, so I blew into his mouth as hard as I could. Pushed down harder on the chest. I didn't know it until later, but I broke two of his ribs. Nothing was working. I was weeping and calling for help, but Tom was out, and our house was too far away for any neighbors to hear.

Finally I gave up on the CPR and ran to the living room to call 911 myself.

It took them eight minutes to arrive.

It was too late.

Not a day goes by when I don't curse myself for not letting that telephone ring. There was nothing so important that it couldn't wait until I drained that bathtub.

As for Gerald, well, I always wanted to think he had nothing to do with it, but neither can I banish the suspicion that weighed on me on that day moving forward. And, well, after everything that has been revealed about his crimes, I'm afraid I know what truly happened.

CHAPTER 5

Amelia

Iowa City, 2024

When I leave Gabby's room, I can't quell the dismay at the thought of her turning those pages. My bedroom is situated on the opposite side of the house from Gabby's, a little effort to give her some autonomy, though at times I worry about having her so far away from me. The walk to my room gives me time to think about what will take place in her head as she's exposed to Gerald's depravities. As I was researching and writing *Beyond the Glass*, I had nightmares the likes of which I had never before experienced. The stories Gerald told, of dressing up his victims like the starlets he admired from the movies and magazines. The thought of those poor women haunted me and always will.

But I've never supported censorship of any kind, and I'm going to have to let go of the notion that I will be able to protect Gabby from everything horrific in real life. All I can do is prepare her for the ugliness that exists in people like Gerald Shapiro.

In my room, I kick off my sneakers and sit on my bed, picking up my phone to see if I missed any calls or messages. A text message pops onto my screen, and my stomach turns over. It's an Amber Alert.

Iowa City girl missing. Bridget Mahoney, age 17. Last seen near Freshly Ground in the Ped Mall. Brown hair. 5'4". 120 lb. Wearing a red puffer jacket and blue jeans. Possibly in a black truck. Any information call police.

Jesus Christ. Gabby and Easton left there less than an hour ago. My mind starts to spin. Gabby wears a red coat. Not a puffer, but still.

I think back to the girl who was found in the ditch so recently, with the garish makeup. That's Gerald's MO. And the other girls, from last summer. Same thing, posed as if they were in a fashion magazine, black-and-blue bruises around their necks. If I didn't know any better, I'd believe he was behind it. What if he has a friend on the outside, someone who is following in his footsteps?

What if they're looking for my daughter?

No.

No. Gerald's in jail.

I'm being paranoid. It's not like they're following my daughter, tracking her every move. I think of the pin she sent me with her location. Could it be that they've somehow infiltrated her phone? Did they take the wrong girl?

He does have a reason to have it out for me. Ever since Isaac, my detective friend, and I worked together to bring him down, I've been worried something like this might happen. Gabby could be out one night, doing normal teenage things, and get attacked, out of the blue. Just like the girl tonight. To reassure myself that Gabby is here, is safe, I call her name, my eyes never leaving my phone.

"What is it, Mom?" I hear her voice before her face pops around the corner, concern etched into her features. Her hair is wet, and she's holding a towel around her.

"Did you just get that Amber Alert?"

She shakes her head. "No, I was in the shower. Why?" Her voice is wary. She knows how these alerts affect me, bringing back all the memories of Gerald Shapiro and the things he did. She looks as though she's getting ready to talk me out of one of my paranoid moods, but no. This time is different. This time it's too close.

I hold out my phone to her, and she grabs it. Her eyes slide over the message, and her eyebrows jump in surprise. "That can't be."

"What can't?" I press my index fingers into my temples. "Did you see this girl?"

She nods, handing the phone back to me. "I said hello on my way in."

"Did you see her leave?"

Gabby shrugs. "I guess so. She was gone when we left."

"Did you see the black truck they're talking about?"

She shakes her head.

"Jesus Christ," I mutter, covering my mouth.

I slide my laptop onto the bed and pull up Facebook, wondering if my neighbors or any of the other parents from

Gabby's school know anything. Easton's mother has posted a "thoughts and prayers" message for Bridget's family. It's gotten 37 likes so far.

I open a new tab and navigate to Instagram and type in Bridget's name. "Which one is she?" I ask Gabby, and she points to a girl halfway down the list of search results. Of course it's not private. I click on her picture and hold my breath. The profile picture is a closeup of her face. She's quite lovely, with dark hair, porcelain skin, and blue eyes. She wears a green flannel shirt over a band t-shirt and has a silver hoop in her nose. If you squint and turn your head sideways, she looks just like Gabby.

I click on Bridget's followers—2,769 people seeing her posts about the books she's reading, the stars she gazed in the night sky, and a few selfies of her attending rock concerts of bands I've never heard of. She has a wide, bright smile, but there is something desperate behind her eyes, perhaps just the inherent insecurity that comes with being a teenager.

The ring of my cell phone breaks me out of my reverie. I pick it up and see Jack's name on the screen. I sigh, thinking I'd rather do anything else in the world than talk to my ex-husband right now. It's not that my husband is a terrible person, though I could certainly picture myself standing solidly in that camp after the affair. It's just that I'm already on overload, with Gabby reading *Beyond the Glass*. I'm overwhelmed with the thought of her learning about the things that Gerald Shapiro did to innocent women. And the knowledge that there's an innocent girl out there, lost to a darkness I'm unfortunately too aware of. Talking to Jack is always stressful, and it's a headache that I don't need right now.

I shoo Gabby away and take a deep breath. "Yes?"

"Amelia!"

His voice booms from the other end of the line, sounding as if he's right beside me rather than curled up on the couch in the apartment he shares with Julia, the twenty-two-year-old girl I found naked in our shower a year ago. The girl who, once upon a time, was Jack's student teacher. The mental image tightens my stomach, and I try to shake it out of my head. At first, I told myself that their relationship would never last, but the past few months seem to be proving me wrong. I have to get past this. I can't feel like vomiting every time I hear his voice.

"Jack," I reply wryly.

"Shut your laptop," he says.

"What are you talking about?" I ask, minimizing Instagram on my desktop.

He knows me too well. It's infuriating, the fact that he can read my mind at any given point in time, but he had me too snowed to ever imagine that he was cheating on me. Though it's true that I tend to be transparent, every emotion announcing itself on my face. It's a detriment in my job, where I have to hide my fear and disgust while interviewing criminals. I wish I could disguise the truth in my voice, that he caught me doing exactly what he knew I would do.

"The Amber Alert," he replies. "I know what you're thinking."

Of course, he's right. I'm thinking of Gerald Shapiro. I'm imagining all the horrific things he did happening to Bridget Mahoney. It's what I do whenever I hear about a kidnapping or disappearance of any kind. There's no cure for the illness Shapiro cursed me with when I spoke with him. It's an ailment I'll suffer for life.

"Okay, okay. You've got me."

A chilling thought crosses my mind. Jack has been teaching at Iowa City High School for the past twenty years. Since English is a required class, he sees most of the students by the time they're sophomores. Does he know Bridget?

"Is she one of your students?"

He is quiet for a long moment.

"She's in my fourth period. Nice girl, but I don't think she was in a good place. She kept missing school, and when she was there, she spent the whole time on her phone. One day I took it away just to make a point, but the next day she was back on it. God, I feel evil, but all I can think of right now is that I'm glad it wasn't Gabby."

I don't want to admit it out loud, but I'm feeling the same way. It seems like a sin to be relieved that it's not our daughter, but I'm fairly sure anyone would feel the same way if they were in our position. I wonder how many parents are counting their lucky stars that it wasn't *their* child.

Feeling guilty, I change the subject. "What time are you coming to get Gabby tomorrow?"

"Um, it might be a bit later than usual . . ."

"Why is that?"

"Because Julia has an appointment. For a sonogram."

I feel like I'm hallucinating.

How could Jack possibly think that having a baby with a girl that is practically a baby herself is a good idea? I imagined that they might shack up for a while, a year at most, not that they'd bring another life into this world. What about Gabby? What's he going to tell her?

"Are you serious?"

"I'm sorry, Amelia. It just . . . happened."

"Oh, I'm quite aware of how that happens."

We both sit on the line awkwardly, waiting for the other one to say something to bridge this canyon between us. It's not that I ever thought we were getting back together, but this has completely solidified that notion.

Jack is going to be a father. Again.

I don't have the energy to process this mentally, so I wind up the conversation.

"So when will you pick Gabby up?"

He clears his throat. "I was thinking about six. Does that work for you?"

"Yeah, that's perfect," I say, already reaching for the end call button with my thumb. I'm itching to get back on the Internet, see if I can find out more about Bridget Mahoney. "I'll see you then, okay?"

"Amelia, wait—"

It's too late. I've already hung up.

If Jack were here, he would take the laptop away and make me go take a bath or go for a walk to get my mind off things. He was good like that. Thoughtful. Intuitive. Sensitive. That is, until he decided to sleep with his former student teacher. It's strange, how you think you know people and they turn out to be capable of things you never dreamed possible.

CHAPTER

6

Beyond the Glass

(A. Child, 2019, pp. 123–124)

Gerald's relationship with his mother was complicated. It is worth examining because many psychoses develop from a poor attachment with parents when a subject is very small. In this case, it began when he was first born.

In early childhood, babies rely upon a parent—namely, their mother—to sate their hunger. This builds trust, that a mother won't let her baby suffer. But if that bond is not made from the beginning, a child may develop an internal avoidance to forming relationships with anyone, because they've learned from an early age that they were the only ones they could truly rely on for their own needs.

According to his mother, Gerald was a finicky eater as a baby. She tried to satisfy him through breastfeeding, but he never did take to it. She spent hours holding him to her chest, but he would just turn his face away and continue crying. Eventually, his mother's milk went dry, and they began to feed him with formula.

Even when they gave him a bottle, he wouldn't take it if he was being held. His parents had to prop the bottle up on a blanket for him to take the formula. He would fuss if anyone tried to pick him up. The only way he was peaceful was when he was left perfectly alone.

As he grew up, his mother said she had the feeling that there was something very wrong with her son. When he was old enough to crawl, he would approach the dog and chew on its tail. The poor dog would yelp and run away from him, but that didn't stop young Gerald. As he became mobile, he set on a warpath to torture all the animals the Shapiros owned. They had to get rid of the dog lest Gerald set it on fire. The cats could defend themselves with their claws, but after one of them ferociously scratched Gerald after being teased, the parents got rid of them as well. And of course, there was the incident with Noah. It was as if Gerald was born with a deep hatred in his heart for all living things.

Things in the Shapiro house were hard. It's difficult for even couples with the strongest relationships to stick together while mourning a child. It seems Tom blamed Vera for answering the phone, while Vera cast her suspicions on little Gerald.

In the end, Gerald ended up with his dad, who has positive memories of their time together:

> *We were bachelors then, Gerald and me. He had a cute little babysitter who watched him until I got home from work. What was her name . . . ? She sat with him for years until he was about nine. Then she claimed he was watching her in the bathroom or some such tripe and quit that night. I figured he was old enough by then to take care of himself.*

Some may argue that leaving a nine-year-old by himself for hours at a time constitutes neglect, but Tom considered it a point of pride, something that would toughen Gerald up, make him more independent. The boy was on his own, sometimes for entire evenings or weekends, whenever Tom found a new conquest or just went on a bender.

Looking back on his childhood, Gerald recalled it as terribly lonely. He spent a lot of time at the library, and he got obsessed with looking at the women's magazines that his mother used to leave lying around at the house. He'd check them out and study them closely, replicating the pictures in drawings of his own. Most of his pictures were of women who resembled his mother. He tucked these into a folder that he kept under his bed to take out and look at when he was feeling down.

As time went on and Gerald went into middle school, his pictures turned more violent. The women in the pictures were burned, stabbed, or chopped into pieces. A concerned teacher sent him to see the school counselor, who invited Gerald's father to come in and discuss it, but Tom never showed up for the meeting.

In high school, Gerald took up photography to document his "projects," which evolved (or devolved, depending on how you look at it) into stalking his classmates and taking pictures of them without their permission or even knowledge. He developed the film at home and cut and pasted the film into violent collages, which he kept until he was finally arrested.

CHAPTER 7

Gabby

Iowa City, 2024

I FLIP TO THE next page and immediately wish I hadn't.
There is a collage of photos of young women, smeared with what looks like a red Sharpie marker. At least, I hope that's what it is. I can't believe that they would publish something like this, something so disturbing. One of the girls has what looks like a spike driven through one ear to the other side. I slam the book closed and throw it on the floor, hand over my mouth, feeling like I might throw up.

I want to call my mom to come and cradle me and assure me that things like that don't really happen. It's all made up, it's fiction. I can't believe that she had the stomach to research a man who would think of things like that, let alone do them, which I know he did because my mother described them in her book. I should have listened to her when she told me not to look.

The red-and-black cover of the book is jarring against my eggshell carpet and pastel walls. I get the feeling it's watching me, like a spider just waiting for the perfect moment to go on the offensive. I push myself off my bed and grab it, holding it like a stinky diaper until I shut it in my bottom desk drawer.

I'd wanted to feel like an adult, be able to really absorb what my mother does for a living. Perhaps it doesn't make sense, but I felt like I'd understand her better. She's been so on edge ever since Dad left, but maybe it has nothing to do with him. Maybe it's her work that is finally getting to her rather than the fact my father's not here anymore.

I get on my computer to get my mind away from that horrible book. I can't take the thought of any more girls in pain. I navigate to Facebook, looking for some comforting pictures or messages. When I log in, there's an old picture of my father and me fishing. It was posted on this day nine years ago, when I was seven. I proudly showed off my four-inch bluegill, the first fish I ever caught. My scraggly brown hair is tied back into two messy pigtails, and I'm missing a front tooth. On my t-shirt, Elsa shoots ice from her palms, creating an intricate castle. I remember how my father would tease me while making breakfast, spinning around with a spatula and singing "Let It Go" until my mother gave him an exasperated look.

Now, I hardly see him. Ever since he moved in with Julia, he's been distant with me, only picking me up when it suits him, often going on long vacations with the woman I suppose will be my stepmother at some point. I dread the thought of going to their place for Christmas Eve, having to suffer through one of her vegan holiday meals.

Sighing, I click away from Facebook and go to my Finsta, the Instagram account that I keep private from my mom because she's always stalking my social media, wary of any predators that might be looking my way. I was raised on "keep your account private" and "don't accept messages from anyone you don't know." It's good advice and all, but it means that you'll never venture out and meet new people and learn about the world. My Finsta contains snippets of the poetry I secretly write after my mom goes to bed. It's bad and it's angsty, but it's mine. Everyone needs a little secret, and my writing is mine.

A text pops up on my phone; it's Easton, my boyfriend. We've been going out for three years now. We met freshman year in homeroom. He's the first person I think to text whenever I have a fight with my mom or get a bad grade or am feeling sad about my parents' split. In return, he is constantly complaining about his older brother, the golden child who aces everything and wins gold medals swimming.

I text him about 98% of the time I'm awake. It might be too much, but he's more than my boyfriend, he's my best friend. We're kind of in our own little bubble most of the time.

> Easton: Sorry, dinner ran long. Ramsey kept going on about taking state this year.
> Me: Did you see the Amber Alert?
> Easton: I don't know. Why?
> Me: It's Bridget Mahoney!

Easton: You're fucking with me.
Me: No, it's for real.
Easton: Man, that's messed up.
Me: I know, right? We just saw her.

I click back to Facebook and scroll through my timeline. A news channel has just posted the information from the Amber Alert, along with a picture of Bridget and a message to contact the police if anyone has information. There are tons of comments already, some people offering thoughts and prayers to her family, others damning the kidnapper to a fiery eternity in hell.

Jesus.

I try not to picture Bridget with a spike through her head, but you know how it is when you try not to think about something. It's all you can focus on. After I tell Easton good night, I lie back on my bed and stare at the ceiling for a long time, just thinking of Bridget and how it's sad that I really know hardly anything about her. I mean, I followed her on Instagram, but that doesn't say much. I try to remember her smile, but I can't recall ever seeing it except for the fake one everyone puts on when smiling on social media. There's nothing but the image of her sitting in the corner of the cafeteria, playing on her phone, her lunch untouched.

Finally, I fall asleep and dream of black trucks.

CHAPTER

8

The Kidnapper

I-80, 2024

Once I stop off at the Iowa River to ditch the girl's phone, I get back on the interstate and drive west. Not too slow, though. Can't risk a copper thinking I'm under the influence and pulling me over for drunk driving. I cruise at a steady 65 miles per hour, though it makes me grit my teeth in frustration whenever I am passed. Another black truck flies up behind me and when laying on the horn doesn't work, he maneuvers his way around me. I don't even allow myself the satisfaction of flipping him the bird. I just can't risk it.

The girl is silent in the back seat, a vague, unmoving lump, although I look back every now and then to make sure she's still out. Chevelle is pumping on the stereo, but it doesn't make her stir. It doesn't take me long to get home, and relief pulses through me when I drive up to the old farmhouse Renee and I bought a few years ago to fix up.

The snow has picked up by now, obscuring the little road that leads to the house, though I've driven this way enough times to know just where to turn, a few yards past the big elm on the left. I navigate the drive expertly and pull up next to the two-story house that reminds me so much of Gerald Shapiro's childhood home that was featured in *Beyond the Glass*. I didn't tell Renee what drew me to it, but I think deep down she knew. When she saw the basement, she must have known. After all, she's obsessed with the book, too.

After pulling my mask back on, I exit the vehicle and circle around to the back. When I open the door and see the girl just lying there, I nod slightly, pleased that she won't kick up a fuss when I carry her downstairs. I gather her in my arms, still in the blanket, and kick the door closed with my boot. I almost slip on the snowy gravel twice, but I manage to make it up the front porch steps without dropping her. I realize it's going to take some finagling to fish out my keys and unlock the door with the girl in my arms, so I set her down on the cold, splintered wood while I get into the house and flip on the light. Everything is just as I left it—a total mess, if I'm being honest. Renee hasn't been home in months, and it shows. Pizza boxes piled up next to the couch, empty beer cans stacked on the coffee table. The bitter cold of the winter evening has settled into my bones, and I long to pour myself a tumbler of whiskey and kick back on the faded brown lazy boy and watch some damn TV. But there is work to be done, and I won't rest until I get the girl set up in the basement.

I return outside and pick the girl up, tossing her over my shoulder. She sure doesn't weigh much, not compared to the others. I prefer a woman with a little meat on her bones, if I'm being honest. But this girl isn't for that purpose. This is purely a revenge mission, a way to get back at that bitch, Amelia, who put Gerald away.

Instead of going into the living room and settling down as I long to do, I carry her through the kitchen to the door that leads to the basement. This time, since I've got her over my shoulder, my right hand is free to open the door. The steps downstairs lead into utter darkness. Flipping the switch, I begin my descent. The steps are steep, but I've gotten used to them, like everything else in this house that hints at its age.

At the bottom of the stairs, I step into a large room that has become my workshop over the past few years. On the left, there is a stained mattress and a bookcase full of old spy novels that was here when I bought the house. On the other side is my work table with all of my tools, which is about the only organized area in the house. Before I heeded my true calling, I was a woodworker, and I still enjoy building furniture in my spare time. There's something about carving an intricate design into the back of a wooden chair that is utterly satisfying, although it doesn't compare with my other creative . . . pursuits.

I lower the girl onto the mattress and pull the blanket off her face. Her hair falls away, revealing a face that I expect to resemble the one on the back cover of *Beyond the Glass*, but that's not what I find. The girl's face is one I've never seen before, one that looks similar to Amelia's daughter, but is decidedly not. Her eyes are a bit closer together, nose a little wider, lips a bit thinner. She has a pierced nose and black makeup smeared above her eyes.

Covering my mouth, I back up a few feet, staring at the girl, trying to make sense of it. I was sure the message Renee sent me was accurate. Gabrielle had been at Freshly Ground with her boyfriend, wearing her red coat. But this girl, she also has a red coat. Her hair is the same shade and length as Gabrielle's.

But she's wrong.

All wrong.

I think back to our interaction in the parking lot. The wind had blown across her face, and then she was walking away from me toward the two cars parked in the corner of the lot, outside the light being cast from the streetlight. Damn it. If I had just taken the time to inspect her face for a single moment, not just assumed I was grabbing the right teenager.

What am I going to do?

CHAPTER

9

Amelia

Iowa City, 2024

I CAN'T SLEEP.
 A glance at my phone tells me it's after three o'clock in the morning, but I can't stop thinking about Bridget Mahoney and where she could be right now. Giving up on sleep, I scroll through her Instagram some more, thinking maybe I can get to know this girl better through her photos. She doesn't seem like the type to fall for any modeling scam like the one Gerald used to convince girls to go with him to work on their portfolios. She's just a regular girl, posting pictures of her dog and a birthday cake she made for her mother. Besides her resemblance to Gabby, I can't think of why anyone would target her.

I should call the authorities with my suspicions about the connection with Gerald Shapiro. I wonder if Isaac, my old friend, is still the head detective at the Iowa City Police Department. I haven't contacted him since Gerald was put away for good, though I sure thought about it when I divorced Jack.

I close my eyes and try to remember the last time I saw him. It would have been back after the sting operation to catch the Catfish Killer, almost ten years ago. I wonder what he looks like now. Would his eyes be the same shade of blue? Would there be smile lines where there weren't before? Would his tawny brown hair be going gray?

Jack had always suspected there was something going on between us back then, when we were tracking Gerald down. Maybe there was a bit of electricity but I just didn't want to admit it. The late nights we spent poring over transcripts of the Catfish Killer talking with his victims, the long conversations we had theorizing about the murderer's identity. It was innocent on the surface, but I can't deny there was an attraction there.

One night when we were sitting in his office, plotting how to bring the Catfish Killer down while drinking a bottle of vintage bourbon that his boss had given him the Christmas before, I think he almost kissed me. We were bent over his laptop, scrutinizing profiles of possible suspects, when I caught a whiff of his cologne—something woodsy with spicy undertones, something so uniquely him—and I turned my head just when he was angling his lips toward mine.

I put my hand on his shoulder and pushed him back gently.

"Don't," I whispered.

We were feeling swept away by the intensity of our cause, I thought.

That's all it was.

After that, things were different between us. We stayed on the case, but it was all business. And afterward, we went our separate ways. It might feel a bit awkward, contacting him again, but I have to do what I have to do, anything to help out with this missing girl's case.

CHAPTER

10

Beyond the Glass

(A. Child, 2019, pp. 11–12)

During my interviews, Gerald described his life after high school. College was not in the cards for him. He had no money, considering his father drank himself out of every job he ever had, so Gerald took a job as a truck driver. The job gave him the excuse to travel and meet women all over the United States. He brought his camera with him and posed at local malls as a famous fashion photographer looking for new talent.

At first, he only took pictures and continued to use them to make his sickening collages. But something inside him was restless, needed more than just robbing women of their images. He needed to control them, and to do that, he had to get them on his own turf. He ended up on a website for aspiring models and searched for someone who lived in the area. When he met a girl who attended a state university close to his town, he arranged to meet her for coffee one day, promising to give her some valuable advice from an industry insider who saw potential in her.

When she walked into the diner, he felt like he had struck it lucky. She was lean and long-legged, wearing a sundress and sunglasses pushed on top of her black hair. She reminded him of Courtney Cox, an actress he'd been obsessed with over the past few years. In our interview, he referred to her as his "dark angel," the one destined to be his first kill.

"I couldn't help but notice you when you posted your pictures," he told her. "Has anyone ever told you that you look just like that actress from *Friends*?" It was a weak come-on, but he was just learning.

In return, the girl laughed. "Let me guess, you want to be *my* friend."

He chuckled and gestured to the camera hanging from his neck. "No, I want to make you famous. I've been looking for a girl just like you."

"And what type of girl is that?" she asked, eyeing his camera.

He shrugged. "A little bit down-to-earth, a little bit exotic. I'm always looking for girls who have an interesting mix of both. What's your name?"

"Maisie." She looked down for a moment and then lifted her head and smiled. "I'm sorry, this is all very flattering, but I'm not sure . . ."

"You don't have to decide now," he rushed in. "I'm staying for a couple of days. Holiday Inn on Maple. Room 112. Stop by if you change your mind."

"Okay," she replied, nodding her head. "Okay, I will."

He went back to his hotel then, and he waited until she came, like he knew she would.

CHAPTER 11

Gabby

Iowa City, 2024

MY ALARM CLOCK goes off at six, even though I've been up for hours, torturing myself by reading my mother's book. I picture Bridget Mahoney, shut up in a hotel somewhere, being photographed and killed.

It's not Gerald Shapiro, though, I tell myself. He's in jail. My mother helped put him there.

I scroll through Bridget Mahoney's Instagram feed and read through the absolute insanity being spouted by the majority of my peers. Most of the posts say things like they're thinking of her and hope she's okay, but some of them are downright nasty. Like, "Who is Bridget Mahoney anyway?" Yeah, she kept to herself, but that doesn't mean she wasn't worth getting to know. Simply looking through her feed, I'm thinking that she was way cooler than anyone knew. Her taste in music is killer and she's taken a lot of pictures of nature, like a completely clear stream running into a little mini waterfall and an image of the full moon, looking like she took it from the roof of her house or something.

The doorbell rings, and I see that it's 7:30.

Shit.

I totally lost track of time. Easton picks me up for school, and usually I look for him and skip out to his car before he has a chance to ring the doorbell. I slip out of bed and run downstairs to answer the door.

Easton is dressed in baggy, ripped jeans with a City High sweatshirt. His shaggy brown hair is falling into his eyes. He does *not* look amused that I'm still in my pajamas.

"I'm sorry," I exclaim. "I know, I know, I know."

"Well, hurry up," he says, coming inside and shutting the door behind him. He follows me up the stairs and into my room. It's a wreck, but Easton has seen it enough times that it doesn't even faze him. He grabs a pile of fresh laundry off my bed and puts it on a chair so he has room to sit. He picks up my phone and sees what I'd been looking at.

"You too, huh?" he asks.

"Have you been looking too?"

"Who hasn't?"

"I can't believe the things that people are saying. They're either completely gushing about how amazing she was . . . I mean, *is*. Or they're saying shit like no one will miss her because no one even knew her. It wasn't her fault that she was shy."

"*Is* shy," he corrects me.

"Yeah, I mean, did you look at her pictures? She has some really cool shots, and I love some of the music posts she did."

"The White Stripes," Easton says. "Her favorite."

"I just think it's so tragic that we didn't take the chance to know her when it was still possible. How many people are there like that, people we could talk to and get to know but we never do because they don't fit in with our friend group or whatever."

"Yeah," Easton says softly. "We should have made more of an effort."

After that, Easton gets quiet and pulls out his phone, so I turn to my closet to pick out some clothes. I'm feeling lazy so I just keep my pajama bottoms on and find a comfortable sweatshirt to wear with it. I pull on my socks and step into some sneakers before going into the bathroom to brush my teeth and wash my face. For a moment, I stand in front of the mirror, staring at myself. I could so easily be where Bridget is. Out of habit, I reach down and finger the gold cross necklace my mom gave me for my confirmation. I close my eyes and think of Bridget, hoping she's still alive.

Easton calls out to me.

"Your dad just texted. Is he trying to get you to be best friends with Julia again?"

I go into my room, pick up my phone, and look at the message my dad sent me, asking me if I'd like to make cookies with Julia this weekend. I make a face.

"Always," I reply, shoving my textbooks into my backpack. "Are you ready?"

"Ready for this . . ."

He pulls me in for a quick kiss, his hand grazing my face.

"Let's go then," I say, pulling away and taking one last look at myself in the mirror.

A lot of people say I'm my mother's clone, with toffee-colored hair and eyes. I won't complain. My mom is gorgeous, but when I look in the mirror all I see is a knobby-kneed kid with practically no boobs. I'm not sure exactly what Easton sees in me, but I'm glad he likes it.

Easton and I hurry down the stairs. My mom is making coffee in the kitchen.

"Do you want some?" she calls.

I feel a pang of guilt. I know that she was up all night, thinking about Bridget, just like I was. She's probably worried, paranoid that the same thing will happen to me. I go into the kitchen and give her a hug. Her eyes promptly fill with tears.

"I don't know what I'd do without you," she says.

I bite my lip. "But it's not me."

"It could have been."

"You can't think this way," I tell her. "Why don't you go back to bed, try to get some more rest?"

She shakes her head vehemently. "There's too much to do. I'm going to call the police station, see if there's anything I can do to help. After all, I helped catch one serial killer."

"Don't go too overboard."

She tries to reassure me she won't, but I know my mother.

When she sets her mind on something, she won't stop until she gets her way.

CHAPTER

12

The Kidnapper

Homestead, 2024

I'M FUCKED.

I sit in my La-Z-Boy with a stale beer, staring at the news, where the picture of the girl that went missing last night reflects the face of the one currently in my basement.

Bridget Mahoney, age seventeen.

Fuck, fuck, fuck.

Someone saw my truck sitting outside the cafe. Must have been a kid from the café taking out the trash or something. They don't mention if they got a license plate, so I'm praying I caught some sort of break there. I didn't see any security cameras where I was, so I should be okay as long as the teenage employee didn't write it down.

Renee is definitely going to rip my balls off when all is said and done, but I have to tell her. I know what she is going to say, what I'll have to do, and I can't help but dread actually hearing it from her mouth.

I hold my phone in the palm of my hand, staring down at the call button. Finally, I muster my courage and press it, cringing as I hear it ringing on her end. It rings once, twice, a third time. For a minute I think she isn't going to pick up, but then I hear her breathless voice.

"Why are you calling me right now? We're not supposed to talk until later."

"Yes, but I need to talk to you now."

Her breath hitches. "What is it? Did something go wrong?"

"You haven't seen yet?"

I've still got the news on, and it's all about "Bridget Mahoney, the girl who was abducted outside of Freshly Ground shortly after 7 PM." But let's be real, Renee doesn't watch the news. She isn't remotely interested in what's going on outside of her world. Which is fine, I like that about her—she doesn't get distracted—but it would be helpful if she had some kind of heads-up. No, I'm just going to have to break it to her.

"Seen what?" Her voice lowers. "You got her, right?"

"Well, sort of . . ." I say, letting my voice trail off.

"What do you mean, sort of?"

It all comes out in a burst. "Well, I have *a* girl! It's just not *the* girl!"

There's a long silence, and I hold the phone slightly away from my ear, anticipating the shriek that will surely be coming. But her voice is calm and measured. She never ceases to surprise me.

"You took the wrong girl." It's a statement, not a question.

"Yes."

"I told you exactly where she was. Do you know how much trouble that could have gotten me into, if I had been caught?"

I hang my head, feeling chastened. "I know. I'm sorry."

There's a light tapping on her side of the connection, and I imagine she's googling the news. I stare at the television screen, imagining her seeing the girl's picture and the footage of the two reporters interviewing the kids who were working at the coffee shop tonight. I am so beyond fucked.

"You're kidding me. They saw you?"

"I don't think they saw me, exactly. They just saw my truck. I don't think they got my license plate or anything."

"Well, thank god for small favors," she says, sighing. "Just let me think a minute."

As I am quiet, waiting for her to come up with something, I hear something downstairs. A banging noise. The girl has awakened. She's still gagged and bound, so I'm not sure how she's making such a racket. I hope Renee doesn't hear, just more evidence of my incompetence, my failure to secure the girl properly.

"You're going to have to kill her," she says quietly.

I knew she was going to say it, but I don't like the answer. Gerald never accidentally kidnapped the wrong person and had to dispose of them to protect his own ass, but then he was a pro. I'm just a sad wannabe, trying to walk in his shoes but tripping the whole way. The girl's death will have to be quick and dirty so I can get rid of her before anyone tracks down my truck. Like Gerald, I like to take my time, enjoy the process, but there's no time to be had.

"Get it done," Renee orders. "And I'll see if I can figure out where Gabrielle is now."

I sigh and hang up the phone, throwing a glance to the basement door.

Best to get it over with.

CHAPTER 13

Beyond the Glass

(A. Child, 2019, pp. 19–20)

WHEN GERALD TOLD me about his first kill, I could feel him dissecting me with his eyes. Gauging my reaction, testing how far he should go with the description. I refused to give him a reaction, taking a sip of my tepid coffee and tucking my hair behind one ear.

"Walk me through it," I encouraged him, pen poised above my notepad. "She came to the hotel and then what?"

He eased back in his steel chair, his laced fingers behind his head, handcuffs dangling. His eyes drooped as though he were reminiscing. The light from the swinging lamp over our heads casts eerie shadows over his features—thick, dark eyebrows over cold, exacting eyes. But he was smiling. Like he was recalling a school dance or a birthday party.

"We had a drink," he said. "Talked for a while. I found out she was majoring in psychology. That caught my interest. I'd always wondered why I had such dark cravings. By the time I confessed my intentions with her, the sedatives I'd slipped in her drink had started to work their magic. She tried to get up from the table and escape, but she only made it halfway across the room. She was no match for me when I moved her to the bed."

"Where you posed her?" I asked, to clarify his modus operandi he'd been working with since high school, fooling women into posing for him only to defile their pictures later in his collages. I was avoiding his gaze, studying my notepad when he spoke.

"Where I strangled her," he corrected me. "And then I was able to pose her any way I wanted. I had a copy of *Vogue* I'd bought at the corner store on the way to the hotel, and I tried out some of their arrangements. It was totally different, moving a dead woman's body. She wasn't stiff yet, either. Her limbs were still warm and supple."

According to Jeff Hotchkin, the police officer who responded to the hotel manager's phone call, Maisie Doherty had been dead for about twelve hours. She'd been strangled and then carefully arranged, her body posed on her side on the bed, right arm draped over her hip as though posing for a photo shoot, which of course was what Gerald was going for.

Once the body had been taken away, Jeff and his fellow police officers searched the room for clues to the girl's identity, but they found nothing but an unused canister of film under one of the beds. Whoever had killed the girl had documented it, a fact that made Jeff feel hopeful that they'd have proof when they tracked down the culprit. He was right, the film did help to pin the murder on him once he was caught, but that wouldn't happen for many years.

When Maisie didn't return to her dorm room that night, her roommate became concerned. She called the police, and they asked her to come in for questioning. As her roommate described her long, black hair, the police put two and two together. Her roommate was asked to identify the girl from a picture, an experience that traumatized the poor girl badly. She told me she couldn't sleep for the rest of that semester and ended up taking off a year to stay at her parents' house to recuperate. When a person is killed, it's not just they who suffer. Everyone who was close to that person loses a piece of themselves, sometimes for good.

Maisie's parents describe her as a beautiful soul, a girl who would do anything for her family, who volunteered at a women's shelter, who took eccentric outsiders under her wing and made them feel loved. Gerald seemed to be one of those outsiders, someone she never should have let in. But sometimes hindsight comes too late to benefit those who sacrificed their lives to a living, breathing monster.

CHAPTER

14

Amelia

Iowa City, 2024

After Gabby leaves for school, I pick up my phone, and my fingers type in the number of the police station. I stare at the phone for a moment before I push the call button and wait for reception to pick up. I ask for Isaac, not sure if I want him to be available or not. But then she says I'm in luck and transfers me. Holiday Muzak plays for a few moments, and I think he's not going to answer, but then his deep voice booms into the receiver.

"Amelia! It's been a minute. How are you?"

Before I can stop myself, I say, "Can you please come over? It's an emergency."

"Where are you?" he asks immediately.

I give him my new address and press end call.

There's nothing to do but wait. I sit down at the kitchen table, not touching my coffee, just staring into space. I can't stop thinking about the red coat. Gabby's red coat. And the one I saw Bridget wearing in her Instagram photos. I can't stop the niggling worry that Gabby is the one the killer meant to grab. When the doorbell finally rings, I am in tears.

I open the door, wiping my eyes with the hem of my sleeve, and Isaac is standing there, hat in hands, looking down. When he catches sight of me, his mouth drops open slightly. He looks the same as I remember. Perhaps his hair has thinned slightly, but his big blue eyes are just as piercing as ever. I break eye contact first and invite him inside.

"Isaac. Thank you for making it here so fast."

I lead him into the kitchen and offer him a glass of water, which he refuses.

He smiles kindly. "I'm good. What can I do for you?"

I sigh, pulling my hair into a messy ponytail. I'm sure I look like hell, after getting little to no sleep last night. "I want to talk about Bridget Mahoney."

At the mention of the girl's name, Isaac's eyes go dark. His face is suddenly all business, and even his stature shifts, as though there's an invisible string pulling him up straight.

"Yes, I'm on it. Do *you* know something about Bridget Mahoney?" he asks.

I lower my gaze. It's hard to put into my words, my feeling that there's something wrong about Bridget's abduction, about the disappearances of several girls in the Midwest in the past few months. Every time another girl goes missing, I feel like the Catfish Killer is smiling to himself in his jail cell.

"I feel like *he's* back somehow. Pulling strings from the inside. It's just all too familiar."

Isaac nods. He is quiet a moment and then says, his voice low, "I know what you mean."

I run my hands through my hair. "You've seen the pictures of her, right? It's not just me? She looks so much like Gabby." I pad over to the refrigerator and retrieve Gabby's school picture from last year. In it, she wears her long hair in soft curls that fall around her face.

He takes the picture from me and gazes at it. "I can see the similarities." He looks up at me to do a comparison. "Actually, she looks just like you."

"That's the problem!" I throw my hands up in frustration. "I know I may be projecting, but this latest disappearance seems pointed, somehow. One of Gabby's classmates? A girl that looks just like her." I pause before voicing the most unsettling part. "You know she was there last night, right?"

Isaac's eyebrows jump in surprise. "She was there? At Freshly Ground?"

I nod, realizing I probably should have called him last night when I found out. She hadn't seen anything strange, so I didn't think about it. But, in retrospect, I feel foolish.

"She sent me a pin shortly before the Amber Alert went out. I keep thinking . . . such crazy things, Isaac. Like what if Gerald is behind all this? What if he's got someone on the outside? What if they meant to grab Gabby and not Bridget? What if they're monitoring her phone and they knew where she was because of the pin she sent me?"

Isaac puts his hands on my shoulders. "That's not what's happening."

"But how can you be sure?"

"Look, I can swing by the school, have a word with her if that will make you feel better. I can even grab her phone and have the guys in the lab run some tests on it, make sure there's no malware that can track her. Does that sound alright?"

I take a shaky breath and tell him yes.

Isaac nods. "I need to go over there, anyway. I'm going to look through Bridget's locker, see if there's anything that can give a clue about why she was taken. I'll just have them call Gabby to the office so I can talk to her."

"Thank you," I say. He is something familiar in this nightmare. I want to reach out and touch his face, feel that he's really here. I want him to hold me and tell me everything's okay, that no one is out to get Gabby.

"I can't believe this is happening again, Isaac. I just can't."

"I know. But trust me, I'll take care of it," he replies, and I notice his hands curl into fists. "Don't worry. I'll find Bridget."

I think of her Instagram account that I found last night. Her wide, innocent eyes. I think of Gabby. If she were missing, I'd want all hands on deck. I have a responsibility here.

"No," I say. "*We'll* find her."

"You're too close to this, Amelia."

I cross my arms over my chest. "It's never stopped me before."

He sighs. "You'd better get your coat."

CHAPTER

15

Gabby

Iowa City, 2024

School on Friday is especially unbearable. Easton and I have PE first period, the same class that Bridget should be in. I catch Easton staring at her spot in line when we take attendance. He catches me looking and shrugs.

"Fucked up," he mouths, and I nod in agreement.

Ms. Paxton seems thrown off as well, because she calls Bridget's name twice before she remembers that Bridget is gone. Her face reddens even more than it usually is.

After attendance, Easton and I start walking laps around the perimeter of the gym. Our pace is slow as we talk in hushed tones about who could be behind Bridget's disappearance. It's not a secret that she'd been seeing the school psychologist for some emotional problems. I'm not really sure of the nature of her issues, but she often comes out of Steven Blair's office with mascara streaked across her cheeks.

"Depression," Easton says. "I'm sure of it."

"If I tell you something, do you swear not to tell anyone else?"

I look around to make sure no one is listening.

Easton links his pinky with mine. "I swear."

"My mom thinks these disappearances have something to do with Gerald Shapiro. She gets super upset every time she hears about one. This time it hit way too close to home. She was pacing back and forth outside my room last night, like she was afraid someone would sneak in and kidnap me too."

I've dropped a bomb, and Easton looks shocked. "How long has it been since she's actually heard from him? I mean, in jail?"

A girl in front of us slows down, and I'm paranoid that she's listening. I hold my finger to my lips until we pass her and put some distance between us.

"Years," I say. "It's been years. I honestly thought that he had died in jail or something, until the killings started happening again. Mom never mentioned him. It was like she was trying to put him in our past. Like she was pretending he didn't exist."

"Jesus," Easton says.

He reaches out to grab my hand, but I don't want people to stare and guess what we're talking about. It's hard enough to be the girl whose mom wrote a tell-all about a serial killer, but today I've been getting more weird looks than usual. Like I have something to do with Bridget's disappearance. Paranoid, I look around to see if anyone's watching us. A girl who was jogging on the other side of the gym trips, and despite myself, I'm relieved to see that all eyes are on her.

Easton's commiseration is nice, but I feel like I need someone else to talk to about this stuff. Not Easton, not my mom, and definitely not my dad.

After gym, I linger outside the counselor's office. Mr. Blair has been busy all day, speaking with students who claim they're suffering trauma from Bridget's disappearance. It sickens me, but that's just the way high school is. As soon as someone dies or something else terrible happens, everyone pretends they had a special connection with that person.

The girl who comes out of Mr. Blair's office is Serena Austen, a girl I knew for a fact would never give Bridget the time of day. She is wiping actual tears from her face, and I wonder if I'm being too harsh. Maybe she had something terrible going on in her life that she was talking about, but when she leaves his office, she says, "Thanks for listening. I just really miss her."

It makes me furious that she'd use Bridget's disappearance as an excuse to garner pity from the teachers, especially Mr. Blair, who had his own business with Bridget.

"Everything okay, Gabby?" Mr. Blair asks when he sees me standing there. He must see the rage on my face. "I mean, really. Do you want to talk?"

It won't hurt, I decide.

After all, he has to keep everything confidential, right?

"Sure," I say.

He holds the door open for me, and I wander into his office. I haven't been in here since I was a freshman changing my class schedule. It's made to be a very warm, homey place, with a wax burner giving the room the scent of peppermint. There are half a dozen throw pillows on a couch across from his desk. I sit down and hug one of the pillows to me, I don't know why. Maybe I feel like I need a shield for this conversation.

"How are you holding up?" he asks. "Were you good friends with Bridget?"

I shake my head. "Not really."

"But you are struggling with this?"

I am quiet, but he seems to understand that I am reluctant to open up.

"What can I do for you?"

I do need someone to talk to. Someone neutral, someone who can give me an objective opinion on what's going on with me.

"Do you know who my mom is?" I say, testing him a little bit.

He furrows his brow. "Amelia Child? Of course I know."

"I mean, about her job."

Mr. Blair clears his throat. "Yes, I've read her book."

"Everyone has," I say. "Which is sort of the problem. I feel like I can't even trust my boyfriend with how I'm feeling right now. It's hard to explain."

My eyes drop from Mr. Blair's face to a picture on his desk. It's a photo of him with a beautiful woman and two small children. It helps me to feel more comfortable with him, to see him as a father figure instead of some guy who listens to teenagers' boring problems. Someone who, unlike my own father, actually cares about people's feelings.

"Try me," he says.

I take a deep breath. "I've just read her book for the first time, and I can't get it out of my head. The things that happened to those girls. I just keep picturing Bridget that way."

Mr. Blair nods. "That's understandable. It doesn't make it better, but I think it's totally natural to be making those connections right now."

His words soothe me, but I'm still wary to go back into the jungle that is high school. The clock says it's almost lunch, and I don't feel like sitting with a bunch of animals in the cafeteria right now. Not even with Easton.

"Yeah," I reply softly.

"Do you want to tell me about these images that you can't get out of your head?" He tents his fingers, elbows on his desk. It's such a shrink kind of gesture, it almost makes me laugh. It takes me a moment to compose myself.

"He liked to take pictures of the women. Gerald Shapiro, I mean. He'd kill them and then arrange their bodies in different ways, like they were models. I keep picturing Bridget's lifeless body, dressed up in something she would never wear, being made to pose for the camera. It makes me want to throw up."

Mr. Blair is quiet for a moment. "That sounds really upsetting."

"And my mom is really freaking out. I know she keeps thinking about what she would do if I disappeared."

Mr. Blair nods. "That makes sense. But you know that won't happen, right?"

The problem is, I don't know that. I keep thinking about how I was there last night. It could just as easily have been me. To my dismay, my eyes start to tear up. I don't want to cry. It's the same reason I got mad at other kids for acting like they knew Bridget really well when I know for a fact they haven't exchanged three sentences with her. But I can't stop myself. And I don't think Mr. Blair can understand my position. Not really.

Mr. Blair pushes a box of tissues forward; I take one and blow my nose. I take a few deep breaths to regain my composure. "It's just so messed up," I finally whisper.

"It is," he agrees. "I know this has to be hard on you, especially since you just read that book. But you have to know that the police are doing everything they can to get Bridget back. Everything's going to be okay."

I sniffle and nod, even though I don't believe him.

There's a knock on the door, and the secretary pokes her head in. "I've got a hysterical mother in the main office. Could you please come and talk her down?"

Mr. Blair looks from me to her and then nods. "Just one sec, Gabby."

I grab another tissue.

He holds up one finger and then disappears out the door, closing it behind him.

I get up to look for a trash can to throw away my used Kleenex and glance down at Mr. Blair's desk. There's a manila folder with Bridget's name on it. My breath catches. I look up at the door, gauging whether I'd be able to take a peek before Mr. Blair gets back.

My curiosity gets the best of me.

I open the manila folder and see some sort of medical report. "Obsessive-compulsive disorder," it reads. There's a doctor's name and a list of the medications she's taking. I'm about to shut the folder when I see a yellow post-it note sticking out of the back. I turn the page to see what it says, and I gasp.

It's my name.

At that moment, I hear Mr. Blair's voice in the hallway. Quickly, I close the folder and dart back to my seat. By the time he opens the door, I am right where I was when he left, although I can't stifle my heaving breaths. I try to make it look natural, like I'm still distraught over Bridget's disappearance and not the fact that my name is in her file for some reason.

"That's it. Just take deep breaths," Mr. Blair says. "Take a moment."

He sits down at his desk, and I'm afraid that he'll notice that the folder moved slightly, but he is more concerned about me. "Feeling better?"

I gulp. "Yeah."

"If you need to come back and talk with me again, I'm here for you. Okay?"

"Thanks, Mr. Blair."

Steeling myself, I rise and walk out into the hall, where I paste a brave smile on my face and attempt to pretend nothing's wrong.

CHAPTER

16

Beyond the Glass

(A. Child, 2019, pp. 23–25)

L ET IT NOT be said that Gerald wasn't a great actor.
He used this talent frequently throughout the years, passing as a pleasant, hardworking member of society. He took a job as a manager at a Holiday Inn on the outskirts of Cedar Rapids, Iowa, and his job evaluations were all top notch. At first.

It wasn't until he let his temper get the best of him at work one day that his facade of easygoing camaraderie would fall apart. He was in the break room with a couple of coworkers when one of them made a "yo' mama" joke about Gerald's mother, whom he hadn't seen in years. He flew into action, punching the other worker right in the face, breaking the man's glasses. Immediately, when he realized what he'd done, he apologized profusely and even talked the coworker out of legal action. He evaded termination by promising his superiors he'd attend anger management counseling.

He sold his therapist, Dr. Nagle, a pack of lies. She thought he was anxious, so that's what he would be. He laughed as he told me about making his hands and his knees shake as if it was from nerves. How superior he felt, playing the role of poor little lamb in a big world, snowing everyone, when he was the biggest wolf of them all.

However, something happened within the walls of that therapist's office. Dr. Nagle helped him to see the value in being vulnerable. Gerald had always thought it was a useless emotion, one that would leave him powerless for others to run roughshod over him, but through her counseling, he saw it now as a tool, a very valuable one at that. If he showed the most tender parts of himself, or at least the imaginary tender parts, the other person might let down their guard more easily.

It was a technique that he used to trick Dr. Nagle, for one. She was a very attractive woman with a blonde bob and curvaceous figure. He made it his mission to show her how to loosen up a little. Of course it went against every ethical rule in the book, but he was very, ah, persuasive, sending her chocolates and flowers any old day in the week.

At first, she was tepid toward his advances. But soon, as Gerald shared his most intimate secrets, his fear of being abandoned like he was by his mother, his deep-seated insecurities from the abuse he suffered from his father—well, no psychologist could resist that. Of course, to do things by the book, she had to wait until they were finished with the mandated anger management sessions, but as soon as their business was finished, the pleasure began.

He took her to an upscale steak house on their first date. One steak cost nearly one hundred dollars, several days' pay for him, but he encouraged her to order as much as she wanted—drinks, dessert, and all. He recalled, during our interview, the chocolate-covered strawberry that he fed her, and how her lips felt around his fingers. How powerful it felt, to have tamed such a self-sufficient woman.

So maybe he didn't care about her.

Maybe he was just doing it out of boredom, just to see if he could. The problem was once he got what he wanted, he immediately wanted something else. He grew bored of Dr. Nagle, which was unfortunate for her. He had never shared his proclivities for the things he did with women when he tired of them.

But she was about to find out.

CHAPTER

17

Amelia

Iowa City, 2024

Isaac and I begin our investigation over Bridget Mahoney's past twenty-four hours by going to the high school. When we check into the main office with the secretary, a man that I remember from Gabby registering for classes her freshman year walks out.

He pauses, as if trying to place me.

"Ms. Child," he finally says.

"Yes?" I reply, wondering how he can remember the parents of all the children he has helped throughout the years.

"I don't know if you remember me. I'm Mr. Blair, the guidance counselor. We met last year, at orientation. Can I have a word with you?" he asks.

I glance at Isaac, who nods.

"Sure," I say, and I follow him back to his office.

"Have a seat," he says, gesturing to a seat opposite his desk.

I sit down and give him an expectant look, wishing he would hurry up and get to the point.

"I spoke with Gabrielle this morning," he says, tenting his fingers.

"Oh?" I think of how she hugged me this morning, reassured me. Maybe she was putting up a stronger front than she really felt.

"It seems that she's pretty troubled about the Mahoney girl's disappearance. Would it be alright if I met with her a few times a week until all this is solved?"

I pause. For a long time, I've been wondering if it would be good to get Bridget into some type of therapy. Now, after she's read my book, I'm leaning toward yes. It can't be easy, realizing the terrible things that happen in this world and that your mother was tangled up in them somehow.

"You know, I think that might be a good idea."

He nods, pleased.

I think of how satisfying his job must be, seeing people in trouble and actively being able to help to ease their pain in some way. I wish that I could take away what Bridget is going through right now. It only makes me more determined to help find her.

I get up to leave, but Mr. Blair holds out a hand, halting me. I sink back into the chair, but all the while I'm thinking that I can't wait to get out of here. I need to be helping Isaac. I need to be taking steps toward getting Bridget home.

"I shouldn't really be saying this, but I think there's something you should know," he says, then hesitates for a moment. He seems to be pondering his next words, and I wonder what more he can have to tell me.

"Bridget Mahoney . . . She was coming to see me about some thoughts she'd been having. I really wouldn't talk to you about this under normal circumstances. I thought we'd been making some progress, but, well . . . The truth is that she was a bit preoccupied with Gabrielle."

"What?" I ask, brow crinkling in confusion.

"Well, she's been going through some depression, and a coping mechanism seems to be a fixation with your daughter. A lot of conversations revolve around her observations of what Gabrielle is wearing or who she's been hanging out with."

My mind swims. Bridget had been focusing on Gabby? Why?

Could this have something to do with Bridget's disappearance?

It just doesn't make any sense.

"Is this something I should be concerned about?"

I'm not sure how he wants me to react.

"No. I don't think so. Lots of girls at this age are preoccupied with their peers. If anything, you should be flattered. Gabrielle has a lot to be envied. She's doing great in school, has lots of friends . . . And again, I wouldn't normally be sharing this information with you, but I thought you should know, given the circumstances. Please don't tell anyone but the authorities. We don't need rumors about a kidnapped girl getting around the school."

I sit quietly for a moment, trying to process this information and how it fits in with everything else that's happened.

"Well, thank you for letting me know," I say, gathering my purse and rising.

He lifts his chin. "I'll make an appointment with Gabby for next week. Let me know if there's anything more I can do for your family."

I give him a weak smile and leave his office, looking for Isaac. I see him standing outside in the hallway, and I start to tell him about this latest information but then I turn my head and see my daughter coming down the hall. She looks how I feel, like she didn't sleep one wink last night. I want to run to her and sweep her up in my arms, smooth her hair, and tell her everything's going to be okay, but of course I don't because she's sixteen and she would probably rather die than hug her mother in the middle of a high school hallway.

"What are you doing here?" she hisses after crossing the hall in a few long strides. I can see that she's been crying. A few streaks of mascara remain on her cheek. I fight the urge to wipe them away for her.

"Isaac needs to speak with you."

She shifts her gaze to the detective standing beside me. She was only seven the last time she saw him. I wonder if she recognizes him at all, the man who used to come to our house and bring her Shopkins to play with while we went over the latest details of the Catfish Killer case.

He smiles. "Hi, Gabby."

She doesn't return the smile.

"I was hoping I could ask you some questions about last night. You and your boyfriend, you were at Freshly Ground when Bridget was, right?"

She nods.

"Great. Do you have a minute?"

Gabby looks at me for a signal, and I nod. "The principal said we could use the detention room to chat. Easton is already in there."

She releases a deep breath and then says, "Okay, sure. Whatever."

Isaac holds the door for her, and I follow her inside. The room is a regular classroom, with rows of desks facing the teacher's desk in the front of the room. Gabby sits down at a desk next to Easton and grabs his hand. Isaac and I turn a couple of other desks around to face them. I try to give them each a reassuring smile, but they look apprehensive.

"Just a few quick questions," Isaac says. "Mind if I record this?" He holds out his phone and looks at me. I shake my head, and Gabby shrugs. Easton looks totally spaced out.

"Perfect." Isaac sets his phone on the desk in front of him and pulls up the voice recorder app before hitting the start button. "Okay, about what time did you two get to the coffee shop last night?"

"Around four-thirty, I think," Gabby says, looking to Easton for confirmation. "We had a math test today, and we wanted to go over our notes." When Easton doesn't respond, Gabby squeezes his hand.

He shakes his head, as though coming out of a trance, and then says, "Uh, yeah. That sounds about right."

Isaac taps his fingernail against the desk, looking thoughtful. "Was Bridget there already?"

"No," Gabby says, eyes flicking over to Easton. "She came in after us. I remember because I heard her order a caramel frappuccino, and I wished I had gotten something like that instead of what I was having." She throws a wry look at Isaac. "I'm not supposed to have sugar during basketball season. Coach says it makes us sluggish."

"Gotcha," Isaac says. "And where was she sitting in relation to you?"

The kids are both quiet for a moment, and then Gabby tells Easton, "Feel free to jump in at any time. You were there, too."

I want to tell her to go easy on him. When Gabby gets stressed, she's a little prickly. But Easton blinks and says, "I don't really remember."

My heart goes out to the kid. He looks positively lost.

"She was on the other side of the shop," Gabby reminds him. "We were sitting in the front, on the little couch, and she was at one of the tables, facing us. I got a little uncomfortable because it seemed like she was staring at us. Or maybe just you."

Easton looks embarrassed. "I don't know why she'd be looking at me."

"I don't know, either," Gabby says. "But she was."

Isaac cuts in. "Uh huh, and how long do you think she was there?"

Gabby waits for a minute, giving Easton a chance to speak, but he's like a deer in headlights. Finally, she says, "I don't know, maybe forty-five minutes? She was messing around on her phone for a long time. It seemed like she wasn't in a hurry. I only noticed her leave because she stopped and said goodbye, and I felt bad, like I should talk to her more, but we were in the middle of studying, so . . ."

Isaac nods understandingly. "That makes sense. And when you left, what did you see?" He gestures for her to continue.

Gabby bites her lip. "Nothing. Well, there was a car near Easton's that wasn't there when we went in. A red sedan. I think it was Bridget's car."

Isaac grabs his little pad of paper out of his front pocket, flips it open, and takes a look. "That's right. A red 2009 Toyota Camry. But you didn't see anyone else?"

Gabby shakes her head. "Nope. That's it."

Isaac flips the pad closed again and stuffs it back into his pocket. "Easton, is there anything else you'd like to add?"

"No, sir." Poor kid looks like he's going to wet his pants.

Then Isaac pulls out a little piece of paper. It's a picture of Easton at an amusement park, taken last year when the freshmen took a class trip for scoring well on the state exams. I'm not entirely sure, but I think it's from his Instagram.

"Do you know why Bridget would have had this picture in her locker, Easton?"

Easton looks like he's going to cry. "Um. We used to date."

Gabby stares at him, open-mouthed. "What? When?"

"In the eighth grade. It wasn't a big deal. Just texts and stuff."

Gabby stares at her hands, and I feel just as blindsided. If Bridget and Easton were together at one point in time, it seems natural that she would be a little curious about Gabby now. What Mr. Blair had to say suddenly seems to make more sense.

Easton lowers his head into his hands. I imagine Easton has a tough conversation in his future. The whole thing is just bizarre to me. Not only does Bridget look so much like

Gabby, but she dated him as well? This has to be more than a coincidence.

"One last thing, Gabby," Isaac says. "Would it be alright if I snag your phone for a little while? Not to scare you, but I want to run a few tests on it."

Gabby looks at me, horrified.

"What, you think someone was tracking me?"

"No, no," I put my hand on hers, not wanting to alarm her. "It's just precautionary."

Gabby stares at me for a minute, then pulls her phone out of her pocket and slides it over to Isaac. I squeeze her hand. "Thanks, baby,"

CHAPTER

18

Beyond the Glass

(A. Child, 2019, pp. 37–30)

IN OUR INTERVIEWS, Gerald Shapiro recalled the murders he committed after Maisie Doherty. Once his father died, he was free to turn the basement into a photography studio. He wanted a place to lure girls with stars in their eyes to their own murders.

It was easy enough.

He created a website with a fake name, a prestigious photographer who preferred to work in the Midwest and search for new talent that might be on their way to Hollywood. Girls loved the idea of putting together a free portfolio to take with them when they went to hit the big time.

Normally, he'd set up a date with them at a coffee shop, and as they chatted, he'd set them at ease with his farm-boy good looks and quick sense of humor. He'd flatter them, saying how beautiful they were and how the camera would just love them. He made them feel lucky to have run into him, that it was their big chance to meet someone so influential. And how kind of him to provide services with the agreement that he'd be able to keep a set of the photographs.

They didn't know that these were his trophies.

He described the first time he brought a girl home to his studio:

> *I set it all up special, made it very modern with white and black furniture and photographs hanging on the walls. I had to display my wares, you see, so they knew I was a great photographer and wasn't just messing with them.*
>
> *The first girl contacted me at my website. Rolfe Wagner. That was the name I used on the website. No one would want to get their pictures taken by some creep named Gerald. I trimmed my hair short and wore pressed slacks and collared shirts with a tie, and the girls ate it up. It absolutely wasn't me, but that was okay. Anything that would get the girls. I had to create an elaborate fantasy in their heads for my ruse to work, and so I did.*
>
> *Anyway, back to the girl.*
>
> *Fiona Redding. See, I never forget a name. I never forget a girl.*
>
> *She was young, about nineteen. Old enough to have seen what awaited her if she stayed in the Midwest. Shitty job for minimum wage, find a guy who*

makes a decent living—a salesman or something—then boom. Marriage, kids, and death.

This girl knew what she wanted, and she wanted out.

I was her key to the rest of the world.

We met at a little cafe downtown, kind of a trendy place that a yuppie would enjoy. I paid too much for our coffees, which had fancy names and even fancier pastries to go with them. She got some sort of latte and I had an espresso.

The talk was the same every time. I had sort of a script I liked to follow. Ask her about her childhood, her dreams, and inevitably they'd talk about hitting the big time. This girl wanted to be a soap star. She dreamed of acting with the stunning people who created beautiful and terrible stories on television.

So I planned on giving her a beautiful and terrible death.

When we got back to my place, she had no reason to suspect that things were about to go awry. Well, she may have had some misgivings about going with a stranger down to his basement. But that's where I had my backdrops all ready and a stool for her to sit on. As I took the first shots, we talked about inconsequential things—the weather, which state college had the best football team. She was wearing ripped jeans and a white t-shirt. She looked very clean, no makeup or anything, just a fresh, blank face. I loved that. I got to create her, mold her into my dream girl.

They were all my dream girls when they were with me.

Eventually, I got enough warm-up shots of her. It was time to play my game, get her to show a little more skin. I was good at talking people into things they weren't sure they wanted to do. Flattery was the most important tool in my toolbox. It only took a few compliments to get her to disrobe for me. Nudes, you know. She liked it.

But soon I got tired of taking pictures. I wanted to take things to the next level. She wasn't hard to talk into things, if you know what I mean. The next thing she knew, she was in my bed. I only had to hold her down at first—she gave up pretty quickly.

Then the real art happened.

I wrapped my hands around her neck and squeezed. It didn't take very long.

I molded her into my dream girl. I'll spare you the details there. You can look it up in the court records if you want. There are even pictures, but I suppose you can't legally include those in your book.

When I was finished, I dumped her in the river. Easy as pie. It was the start of my routine.

CHAPTER 19

Amelia

Iowa City, 2024

Isaac and I sit in his squad car and stare at the house before us. It's just like every other house on the block. Two stories, picture window out front, fenced-in backyard to keep the dog from wandering too far.

Bridget's house.

I am still struggling to put together the story that Easton told us at the high school, that he had "dated" Bridget in the eighth grade, before Gabby knew him. He didn't know why Bridget would have his picture now; he thought all of that was in the past and was deeply troubled to know that she may still have had feelings for him. I have no idea what's in store for us when we go through Bridget's room, but we have to go see, in case there's any clue about why she would have been targeted as the victim of a crime like this. I'm hoping there are no more pictures of Easton.

There are two vehicles in the driveway, a silver pickup truck and a little green hybrid car. Of course both of her parents stayed home from work. I can picture Bridget's mother, with dark circles beneath her eyes, having not slept all night long—at least, that's what I would look like if Gabby went out for some coffee and didn't come home. Hell, she's not even my daughter and I'm beside myself.

Isaac gets out of the car and waits for me on the sidewalk. As Isaac's the official detective, I follow his lead, but we both agree it's good for me to be there, to offer a bit of emotional support, mother to mother.

As we approach the house, I notice a room upstairs with purple-and-white striped curtains. A lump forms in my throat. They're the same curtains we got for Gabby when we repainted her room last summer.

We climb the stairs and ring the doorbell. There's a Christmas wreath hanging from the door, and a wooden snowman is propped to the right of the door. A face appears in the window, Mrs. Mahoney checking us out, even though she knew we were on the way. When she verifies we are not nutjobs or reporters, she goes to the door to unlock it and pull it open. She stands there in a rumpled nightgown and robe, fuzzy slippers on her feet. Her hair is matted to her head, and her eye makeup has migrated to her cheeks.

"Mrs. Mahoney, I'm so sorry you're having to go through this," Isaac says, and the warmth in his voice seems sincere. "We'd just like to ask you some questions to make sure we're on the right track with the investigation. I'm Isaac Feldmann, and this is Amelia Child. She has a daughter in Bridget's grade."

"Rachel," she says dully, extending her hand.

We take turns shaking it.

She opens the door wider, then ushers us into the living room and motions for us to sit down. It is a comfortable room with cushy chairs and a muted blue color on the walls. I spot a picture of whom I assume is Bridget when she was small, dressed in a little white dress, fit for first communion or some other formal occasion. Mrs. Mahoney catches me staring at it, and her face seems to literally fall, her cheeks and her lips turning downward.

She sits on the love seat and laces her fingers together as if to keep them from fluttering away from her. I notice that she's shaking, but I'm pretty sure it's not from the cold that followed us inside. It's as though her warmth has been stolen; her heart ripped out of her.

"Can you tell us what happened, from the beginning?"

"There's not much to tell," she says, spreading her hands helplessly. "She said she was going to do some homework. I was at work, not here to cook dinner, so she said she'd grab something there. It was nothing out of the ordinary. Until she didn't come home. She didn't answer her phone when we called, and then Mark went to the coffee shop to ask about her. They said she had left an hour earlier, but her car was still there. The only clue they gave was that there was a black pickup truck idling in the parking lot for a while. One of the employees saw it when he was taking out the trash. Then he went to the police station, and the Amber Alert went out."

"Let's backtrack a little," Isaac says, pulling out a tiny notebook from the front pocket of his uniform. "What has her mood been like lately? Any shifts or changes that you noticed?"

Mrs. Mahoney looks down at her hands as if she might find the answers there.

"I'm not sure, really," she says. "She's always been a bit morose. We took her to the doctor a year ago to check for depression after a bad breakup, and she's been on medication ever since. Also a touch of OCD. She develops interests and then dives into them whole hog. She doesn't have a lot of friends. She spends a lot of time on her phone."

I wince at the word *breakup*. It doesn't seem realistic that a girl could be so broken from a mostly text relationship—according to Easton—that she would be clinically depressed about it. Of course, I haven't been a teenager in thirty years. If I thought back to my crushes from early high school, maybe I'd feel differently.

The OCD thing, well, I don't know how to feel about that. Could it be that she was obsessed with Gabby? I think of the red coat and wonder if it's a coincidence.

Isaac writes down the terms *depression* and *OCD* and underlines them twice. "Was she on the Internet any more than usual? Had she met anyone new? Someone she may have spent a lot of time talking to recently?"

I know what he's thinking. If this is really a copycat, the culprit would have groomed her online, just as Gerald did with his victims back in the day. I turn to hear Rachel's answer.

She thinks for a moment, then shakes her head. "Nothing has been really different. At least, not that I noticed. Do you think she knew the person who took her? That she'd met him online?" She drops her face into her hands. "I wish I could remember."

My heart breaks for her.

"This isn't your fault," I tell Mrs. Mahoney. "I'm constantly alarmed by what my daughter is doing online. She's precocious, you know?"

Her eyes shine. "Does your daughter know Bridget?"

"She said she saw Bridget around, but she didn't really talk to her," I reply.

Mrs. Mahoney sighs. "I wish she had."

"Me too," I assure her, leaving out the fact that Gabby is dating Bridget's ex-boyfriend. That would have complicated a possible friendship, for sure. Maybe if she had been friends with Gabby, it would have demystified her a little. She wouldn't have been preoccupied with a girl who had seemingly taken her place.

"Is your husband around?" Isaac asks.

"He's sleeping, finally," Mrs. Mahoney says. "Do you want me to wake him up?"

Isaac looks like he certainly would like her to wake her husband up, but he shakes his head and says, "We can get his testimony later. In the meantime, is there any way we could get Bridget's computer?" Isaac asks, suddenly all business.

"Of course." Getting to her feet with a slight groan, she pulls her robe closer around her, as if a chill has just entered the room. "Come on," she said, gesturing for us to follow her.

The upstairs hallway has three bedrooms and a bathroom. We pass by what I guess must be the master bedroom, as the door is closed and we hear faint snoring. There is an office with a desktop computer and printer. The room at the end of the hall is periwinkle with some silvery tassels hanging around the corners. It is clear that Bridget is artistic, with drawings tacked to her bulletin board. The other thing I notice is how many books are in stacks all around her room. I wander in, taking in all the titles. She has the typical teenage paperbacks, but she also has historical fiction, nonfiction books on caves found in Iowa, and comic books galore.

Isaac locates her laptop on her desk and grabs it and puts it in a plastic bag. As we are turning to go, I glance at a pile on her bed and freeze.

A school library book. The red cover. The title in contrasting black.

Beyond the Glass.

No. I refuse to believe it. There must be a perfectly natural explanation for why Bridget checked my book out from the library right before she disappeared.

Maybe it's just a coincidence.

Or maybe Bridget had gotten it because of the connection with Gabby. Was she looking into my daughter's background by checking out my book? Trying to understand what it was about Gabby that drew Easton to her? My heart clenches when I think of Bridget reading the book, trying to figure out what made the girl who took her place tick.

Mrs. Mahoney must sense my panic because she sets her hands on my shoulders, which seem to be shaking. "Are you okay?"

I clear my throat and say, "Yes."

"What is it?" Isaac asks. He follows my gaze to the book on the bed, and his eyes widen as he looks back toward me, realizing the implications. Reading my book got this girl in trouble somehow. That's the only explanation.

"Could we . . . could we take this, too?" I pick the book up by the corner, as though it will come alive and bite me.

"I don't see the relevance, but take it if you must," Mrs. Mahoney says, already turned away. She clearly doesn't recognize me as the author.

Her movement is painfully slow, and I notice for the first time how fragile she looks. I promise myself that I will do anything in my power to find out who's behind this.

Anything.

CHAPTER

20

The Kidnapper

Homestead, 2024

I WAKE UP WITH a start.

My head aches from the beers I pounded after talking to Renee. I wasn't ready to go downstairs and deal with the girl. I just wanted to be blissfully oblivious until I'd gotten some sleep and could think about how I need to go about this.

The light pouring through the window is full and yellow, not the meek early light of morning. I confirm the time by glancing at my phone. It's nearly noon, and I've missed thirteen calls from Renee, probably to make sure I've gotten rid of the girl. I vow to go downstairs and take care of business before I call her back.

But first, breakfast.

I'm ravenous, having skipped dinner last night. I pad into the kitchen and stare blankly at the dishes piled up in the sink. When I open the cupboard, I find a clean plastic bowl and go to the fridge to get out the milk. There's a little Cap'n Crunch left, so I dump that into the bowl and sit down at the table.

All is quiet, peaceful.

I can almost pretend that I didn't fuck everything up last night and it's just a normal day, one where I can putz around in the basement, working on the bureau I've been restoring for when Renee moves into the bedroom upstairs with me. I thought it would be a romantic wedding gift, a place for Renee to put her sweaters and unmentionables rather than struggle for room in the closet among my stained t-shirts and jeans. What I would give to crank some Stone Temple Pilots and just lose myself in the work.

I close my eyes, holding on to this daydream until a banging noise from downstairs shatters my bliss. Once more, I wonder what the girl could possibly be doing to make the noise. It gets on my nerves enough that I toss my dirty bowl into the sink with the others and cross the room to the basement door. My head starts to pound again. I pause for a moment before throwing the door open and screaming down the stairs.

"You'd better knock it the fuck off!"

The noise stops for a minute before picking up again, full throttle.

I grab my mask and pull it on, then flip on the light and stomp down, my eyes flicking over to the mattress where the girl lies. She's wiggled around so she can kick the bookshelf. There's a pile of spy novels that have been knocked to the floor. She turns her face toward me and then, deliberately slams her feet into the shelf again.

"I said knock it off." I bolt across the room and grab a handful of her dark hair, yanking hard. She moans, her eyes rolling into the back of her head. In the light of day, I can't believe I wasn't able to tell this girl apart from Gabrielle. She's considerably less pretty. Not that it matters. I didn't grab this girl for my own satisfaction, anyway.

I turn toward my workspace on the other side of the room and ponder the tools spread out on my bench. The girl follows my gaze and, seeing the saws and carving kit, whimpers. The sound sends a thrill down my spine. I may not have seized the girl on purpose, but it's still exciting, how she quivers at the sight of my tools.

I push a strand of hair out of her eyes, almost tenderly. "Don't worry, sweetheart. I'm not going to hurt you . . ."

Her wild eyes study my face, gauging my words, and I can see that she's trying to determine whether I'm being honest.

"Yet." I sneer at her.

I sit back on my heels, considering the situation. Maybe this doesn't have to be a mistake. Maybe I can make it work in some way. We could get some cash out of the parents before I put her down. God knows that we'll need the money, especially once we start thinking about a family. I consider the girl. She's wearing ripped jeans and a flannel shirt beneath her red coat, which doesn't scream rich to me, but the kids these days dress that way, whether they've got money or not. Who's to say her parents aren't loaded?

I smell something bad and wrinkle my nose. The girl has made a mess. If I'm going to keep her around, I've got to do something about that.

"Need to go to the bathroom?" I ask.

She just stares at me.

I walk over to my work bench and pick up a carving knife. The girl squeals through her gag, and I can't help but relish the sound. Closing the distance between us, I brandish the blade and sink to my knees beside her. She holds her breath as I lower the knife to the duct tape wrapped around her ankles. It takes one quick slice to get through the tape. I yank the rest of the binding off and stand back up, lifting her with me. She stumbles, like a baby deer on her weak legs, but eventually she gets her footing, and I lead her toward the stairs.

We'll get her cleaned up.

And then I'll decide what to do next.

CHAPTER 21

Gabby

Iowa City, 2024

Easton has the heat cranked up as high as it will go, but I can't stop shivering.

The parking lot has mostly cleared out by now, but there are still a few cars here and there, students staying after school for clubs or sports. It's Friday afternoon; normally we'd go to the mall or a bookstore to hang out, but I don't feel like going anywhere with Easton until he explains himself to me.

He is fiddling with his phone, trying to get his Bluetooth to hook up with the old car's stereo, but not having much luck. I lick my lips, trying to moisten them, but they immediately dry out once more. I grab Easton's tube of Burt's Bees from the center console and smooth them over my lips, the taste reminding me of Easton's kisses, which just pisses me off even more. Does Bridget associate lip balm with Easton's lips or is it just me?

"Tell me again," I say. "What happened with you guys?"

Easton runs his fingers through his dark hair and sighs. "It wasn't even like that, Gabs. We were in the fucking eighth grade. It was mostly just late night texting and sending each other stupid memes and stuff."

"So why didn't you tell me about her?"

"Because it happened a million years ago."

"Two. It happened *two* years ago."

"Yeah, we've been together almost two years, compared to the few months I talked to Bridget in middle school. Gabs, I was playing Minecraft until the eighth grade. It was really nothing." He reaches over to grab my hand, rubs his thumb over my knuckles. I feel myself starting to thaw out a little.

"If it was nothing, why did she have your picture stuck in her math textbook?" That's where Isaac found it, my mom said. He was pulling out her textbooks, and it fell right out. A picture of Easton that Bridget must have taken the time and effort to print from his Instagram. It reminds me of the pictures Gerald would print out of his classmates and make those disgusting collages. My stomach turns.

"I honestly don't know."

Easton reaches out and touches my face, turning my chin toward him with his thumb and forefinger. He leans toward me, and I swat his hand away and look out into the parking lot, watching Ms. Benning, the librarian, walk out to her car. It makes me think of how Bridget spent so much time there, hanging out during lunch instead of going to the cafeteria. I wonder if she's heard about Bridget or has any insight about where she might be. Before I realize what I'm doing, I've opened the passenger door and am walking across the parking lot toward her.

Behind me, I hear Easton getting out of the car to follow me. "Gabs? What are you doing?"

Ms. Benning is putting a box of books in the trunk of her car. When she slams it shut and turns around, she jumps a little to see me standing there. "Hi, Gabrielle. Do you need something?"

I'm not really sure what to ask her, not even sure what made me confront her like this. It just seems like, if I'm trying to learn more about Bridget, this woman would be the one to ask. A librarian is like a therapist in a way; they always know what's going on in people's minds, based on their reading material.

"Ms. Benning? Um, I'm sure you heard that Bridget Mahoney went missing last night. She spent a lot of time in the library. I was just wondering if you knew if there was . . . anything going on with her?"

The woman tucks a strand of red hair behind her ear. She's pretty, for a teacher. Not too old—she's probably been out of school a couple of years, but not long enough to have lost what makes her young. I think maybe that's why Bridget was able to relate to her so much, because she's still young enough to understand teenagers.

"Gabrielle," she begins.

"Gabby, please," I correct her. Most teachers know that I like to be called this, but the librarian never really seemed to pick up on it.

"Gabby." She gives me a tight smile. "I know that you're going through a lot lately. You were there last night, weren't you?"

I'm taken aback. I didn't know that it was public knowledge that I was at the coffee shop last night when Bridget was taken. "Yes..."

"You must be so shaken, thinking it could have been you..."

Her words send a chill down my spine.

She goes around to the side of her car. "You can't let yourself think that way, honey. I don't know for sure, but Bridget was making some poor choices, if her reading material was any indication."

"What do you mean?" I ask.

She opens her car door. "You know I order most of the materials for the library. If I'd been around when your mother's book came out, I wouldn't have ordered it. Simply not appropriate for high school students. But your father insisted we have a copy of it. He's so proud of your mother. But I can't help wondering... why someone like Bridget would go missing after reading something like that. Maybe she got some bad ideas. Maybe she went messing with the wrong sort of crowd after reading about the horrific things that man did." She climbs inside.

My mouth drops open.

Easton puts his hand on the small of my back, sensing my astonishment. "Come on, Gabs, let's get you home."

I watch her car pull away, and the questions on my tongue vanish with her.

CHAPTER 22

Amelia

Iowa City, 2024

Bridget's computer is open on my dining room table. The day has faded into afternoon, and shadows stretch across the hardwood floor. I make coffee for Isaac and set out a box full of donuts we picked up on the way back to my house.

Bridget's mother gave us the best guess at her password—her cat's name, Katniss, and her birthday. I hold my breath as Isaac types in the pet's name. The login screen shakes and then tells us that the password failed. He types in her birthday. No luck.

Isaac bites his lip. "We probably have one more try before the computer locks up." He looks up at me. "What do you think?"

I shrug helplessly, thinking about what we saw in her room—the artwork, the books on Iowa caves, the comic books. Nothing stands out as being worthy of a password. But then I remember her copy of my book.

I take a shot in the dark. "Gerald Shapiro?"

Isaac's eyes widen, and he nods excitedly. "Good one. Just Gerald, do you think, or his whole name?"

There's no way to know, but we've got one guess, and I don't want to waste it. "GeraldShapiro, one word," I finally say, hoping against hope that I'm correct. I hold my breath as Isaac types in the password, and when her desktop pops into view, I let it out in a huff.

Clapping me on my back, Isaac says, "I'd better be careful. You'll have my job in no time." I force a smile and turn my attention back to the computer.

"Social media," I insist. "Maybe someone was stalking her, knew that she was going to Freshly Ground last night. He could have been waiting for her. Maybe she even planned to meet with him, not realizing his bad intentions."

If she had planned a meeting, then it couldn't have been someone looking for Gabby. I don't know what to wish for, that she met someone online and was planning a rendezvous or that she was snatched by accident, the kidnapper thinking she was my daughter. Both are horrible scenarios.

Isaac shakes his head. "First thing we need to do is search for her phone. It wasn't found anywhere on the coffee shop property, so she might still have it with her. If we go into Find My Phone . . ."

He clicks a few buttons and is in Bridget's Cloud account in no time. He pulls up the app, and a map appears on the screen. She has three devices designated to her account. Her computer shows up at my address, her AirPods are at her home, and her phone . . . there is no location found.

Isaac doesn't look surprised. "The guy probably dumped it somewhere. It was a long shot." He closes the window, and we stare at her desktop.

Bridget's files are all very neat, arranged in rows with folders named things like "Bio" and "Pre-Calc." Her Instagram looks completely normal, no suspicious messages from random guys looking to hook up. Unless she's deleted them, in which case we're out of luck in finding out if anyone was trying to groom her or meet up with her.

Nothing really looks suspicious until we pull up her search history. In the last week, she's searched for "Gerald Shapiro's childhood home," "Gerald Shapiro's photography website," and "Where is Gerald Shapiro now?"

Isaac pulls up a website I've seen before called "Free Gerry," a bunch of nutjobs who believe that Gerry is innocent. I know about it because they published some wack-job article about me framing him a while back. It always pops up when one searches about Gerald Shapiro. It seems Bridget read it too. I cross my hands over my chest as Isaac reads it aloud.

"Amelia Child is to blame for all these murders. She planted evidence and turned it over to the police to create a frenzy of people on a manhunt for Gerald just to create a villain for *Beyond the Glass*, painting Gerald as the bogeyman."

I shake my head. "Such bullshit."

We navigate to Bridget's Reddit account, where we see that she took part in multiple true-crime communities, asking about the details of Shapiro's crimes.

"Why was she so interested in Gerald Shapiro?" I ask Isaac, thinking of the copy of my book on her bed. I think of my own copy of *Beyond the Glass*, floating somewhere around Gabby's room. Again, I am staggered by the fact that my daughter could just as easily have been taken. Add in the murders that have been happening recently in the area, and it all adds up to a picture that I feel so close to seeing but hasn't come together for me yet.

We spend some time looking through her other social media and don't find much else to speak of. I think about where I kept stuff from my parents when I was a teenager. There wasn't so much technology. Instead of the texts the kids send to their friends, back in the day we passed actual notes with our gossip. I hid them in my closet in a shoebox beneath a pile of shoes, along with my diary.

Maybe Bridget has her own proverbial shoebox somewhere on this computer, somewhere innocuous where her parents would never think to look. I gaze at her desktop and click on one of her school folders. The first one yields nothing but math notes. The second one is notes for a history exam. But the last folder, labeled "English," contains a journal.

"That was clever of her," I tell Isaac. "I was always nervous about my parents finding my journal, back in the dark ages when we had to use a pen and paper."

"I never kept one," he replies. "But I'm glad she did."

The two of us spend an hour or so going through her journal entries, which reach back to her freshman year of high school. Her entries are what you'd expect a teenage girl's diary to be ... insecurities about starting high school, her crushes on boys, and her lamentations that she didn't have many friends. Any friends, really. In her words, she had people she said hi to, but no one she could open herself up to, for fear of being made fun of. She saw herself as a freak, so depressed all the time that she couldn't relate to anyone.

One of her most recent entries caught my attention. She didn't use actual names, just pronouns, which I guess makes sense if someone got ahold of this somehow. It was written at the end of November, just before Thanksgiving break.

> *He sat across from me at lunch today. Well, across the cafeteria from me, but I watched him just the same. He was with her again. They seem to be together all the time now. I can't keep from being a little jealous. The easy way they have with each other. He picked up her corn muffin and just started eating it, while she grabbed his soda and took a slurp. I wonder what they're like when they're alone, if they have that kind of intimacy in public. Like, does he tell her all his secrets? Does he tell her about us? What I would give to listen in. So many questions.*

"Holy shit," I say. "She's talking about Gabby and Easton."

Isaac nods. "Probably."

The entry seems a bit unhinged to me.

But it has nothing to do with her disappearance.

Does it?

Finally, Isaac closes the laptop and slips it into his briefcase. "I've gotta go to the station. I'll have Allen go through this and come up with a report."

"Should I come with you?" I ask, disliking the idea of being alone at this particular moment. I want to feel like I'm doing something productive, and sitting around and doing my nails doesn't quite fit the bill.

Isaac stops and looks at me for a moment. "You okay?"

I inhale deeply and release a jagged breath. "I just don't think I'll be able to relax until she's back home with her parents."

He gives me a look filled with empathy, and I know that he's remembering those times that we worked on Shapiro's case together, so many years ago. He knows how invested I get, unable to let go of a puzzle until I have every last piece sorted out.

"I'll call you," he says softly, brushing a strand of hair out of my face. "Okay?"

The tenderness nearly undoes me. It frightens me, how much I want him to pull me close and comfort me. He's known me so well for so long, and vice versa. Every little thing he does brings back echoes of yesteryear. I haven't felt this close to anyone since Jack and I split, and the idea that I could open myself to someone else again and risk getting my heart trampled once more is more than I can bear.

"Okay," I reply, pulling away.

Maybe it's better that we take a few hours apart, some time to cool down. He smiles and hugs me before grabbing his briefcase and leaving.

When he leaves, I am left sitting at the kitchen table, staring into space. The room is silent, and yet I feel unsettled, as though I'm not alone. Eventually, I realize that it's Bridget's copy of *Beyond the Glass*, laying a few inches away, that feels like the presence of another person in the room.

I pick it up and flip through the pages. It naturally falls open in the middle, where the spine seems to be broken, like someone set it upside down and cracked it by accident. There's a picture of one of Gerald's victims.

My mother.

CHAPTER 23

Beyond the Glass

(A. Child, 2019, pp. 41–47)

Now comes the hard part.
 I can't think of anyone else who would want to sit down with their mother's killer and question him about his motivations and what actually happened that day, but it was important for me to contextualize my mother's death. It's the reason I undertook writing this book, to try to understand this individual who found pleasure in taking other people's lives.

Around the time Shapiro met my mother, he had branched out from chatting up would-be models on the Internet. He met her on a grief support board after she lost a pregnancy and was working through her miscarriage. He claimed that his wife recently passed away, and she expressed her sympathy, encouraging him to share his feelings. My mother was always one to lend a listening ear to someone going through a hard time, and she treated Shapiro no differently. When he suggested that they meet in person, she agreed. It was in the early days of the Internet, and people weren't as aware of the danger as they are now. Her kindness was her undoing.

From his journal:

I saw her right when I walked in. It honestly made me bristle a little because I usually like to show up first so I can scope it out and choose a seat where I can see the door, where I can plan a quick exit if I need to. There's also something about watching a beautiful woman approaching me that I love.

It's different when you're walking toward them. I felt less in control somehow. A little paranoid. It made me feel like I was presenting myself and waiting for her approval.

I'd much rather be the one deciding whether she's worthy.

But from my vantage point, she was definitely a fine specimen. She was wearing a scoop-neck black top with a black choker. Her dark, curly hair fell softly around her face. Her dimples appeared when she saw me coming. She was breathtaking.

She rose when I stood next to the table, and I showed how unnecessary the gesture was by waving my hand and sliding into the booth across from her.

"You're early," I said, passing my hand through my hair and flashing a grin.

"I know," she replied, her voice sweet as tupelo honey. "My husband left for the gym, and I was ready, so I just . . ." She trailed off. "I like to be punctual."

The mention of her husband stirred a black cloud in my head, but I tried to keep my smile in place. The smartest way to conceal insecurity is by turning the focus away from yourself, so I forced myself to ask her some questions about her family.

"The gym, huh?" I wondered what his face looked like, how it would look with my fist pounding into it repeatedly. I liked a challenge.

She laughed. "Yeah, he has free access to the gym since he just volunteers at CHC."

"CHC?"

"Yeah, City High Campus. It's the local high school. He collaborates with the head high school coach and takes teams to run drills when the coach is working with the kids one on one."

"That's . . ." I struggled for the right words. Pathetic? A waste of time? "Admirable."

The compliment seemed to please her because her cheeks tinged just a little. I wanted to see her face even redder, and not with pleasure. But I pushed these thoughts out of my head, determined to do the work to deserve my reward.

"And what do you do?" I asked, leaning forward, so interested, eager to get to know everything about her. People like to talk about themselves, almost always, with the ones who don't (like me), being the ones you want to avoid. The more information you give about yourself, the more ammo your enemy has against you.

Not that Elaine was any match for me, and she wouldn't be around much longer anyway.

"*I work at a shelter. We take in people who've been abused until they can get back on their feet. We help them find jobs if they need them. We're kind of a one-stop shop.*"

My interest actually perked up. "*Oh, yeah? That's really noble of you. Do you volunteer or do they pay you?*"

"*We work on donations mostly, but yeah, the government gives us a meager amount. I make a little. Enough to pay the bills. Or some of the bills. My husband works in banking, so he makes the majority of our income.*"

I nodded, thinking a shelter would be filled with all sorts of damaged women. It was like my mecca . . . if only I could get her to share where it was.

"*I'd love to volunteer doing something like you do at the shelter. My dad used to hurt my mom, but she was able to get away. I think it's so important to make escape possible for people feeling trapped and broken.*"

Inwardly I applauded myself. When I wanted to, I could bullshit with the best of them.

"*That's so nice!*" *She cocked her head to the side, appraising me.* "*I could give you the phone number. The head of the program is Tracy—she's really cool. I'm guessing she'd love the extra help. We do a lot of moving heavy furniture when one of our ladies moves into her own place. My husband usually does some of it, but we can always use an extra pair of hands.*"

"*Perfect,*" *I told her, channeling my most angelic smile.*

Elaine took her purse into her lap and rummaged through it, finally coming up with a purple ballpoint pen.

"I don't think I have any paper," she said.

"Just write it on my hand," I said, holding my palm out, face up. She laughed a little and then leaned over, carefully printing the numbers on my hand. I blew on the palm of my hand, not wanting to sweat and lose the number.

At that moment, the waiter came over with a pad of paper. His arms were ripped and covered with tattoos—the silhouette of a curvaceous woman, the head of a lion, a skull and crossbones. Typical, unimaginative tripe. If I was by myself, I'd make a sarcastic remark about how unique they were and ask where he got them. But I wanted to impress Elaine, make her think I wasn't just a nice guy, but the nicest guy.

"Cool tats, man," I said, expecting him to thank me.

Instead, he gave me a long look, long enough to make me feel uncomfortable, and I'm not the sort to get uncomfortable. But I got the feeling he could see inside me, see what I was capable of. I wanted to follow him back to the kitchen and stab him until he bled out.

Elaine didn't seem to have noticed any of this. She had gathered up the menu, studying it intently. Finally, she ordered a house blend with two sugars and some creamer.

He wrote down her order. My eyes scanned his nametag. Toby.

I told him that I'd have the same.

He gave me no verbal response, which infuriated me. He simply made a note on his little pad of paper and turned around to fetch our drinks.

I shook it off. I couldn't afford to lose concentration. My next move was to discuss our purported reason for the meeting. I'd rehearsed my speech in the car, inventing the details to make my tragedy believable.

"It's been a hard day," I said, pushing my napkin around in little circles. "It's actually the anniversary of my wife's death."

"Oh no," Elaine prompted. "How are you holding up?"

"I'm just depressed. No matter what I do, there's no fixing the hole she's left in me. Doctors, medication, you name it. Nothing seems to work."

Elaine's forehead wrinkled with concern. "I'm sorry. You could have called me to say you were staying home. I wouldn't have held it against you."

I held up my hand, as if to brush aside her concern. "It's better that I'm with someone."

She sighed. "Still, I feel awful. I've been there. I know how it feels. I mean, not to lose a spouse, but I've definitely felt the hole a death leaves behind. For me, it's the death of hope. I so wanted a sibling for my Amelia. Of course we'll try again, but it doesn't take away from the loss, even if we get pregnant again."

"I totally get that," *I told her and reached across the table to graze her knuckle with my fingertips.* "Each child is unique."

Looking uncomfortable, she pulled her hand away.

After that, I focused on her, getting her to share the story of her woe. I tucked away each weakness that she shared, cataloging them for future use. Not that I'd need the tidbits for very long, but it was a force of habit. Just something I do when I'm listening to someone.

When we finished our coffee, she looked at her watch. I remembered that she had a family dinner scheduled later, but it was only 2. I thought surely she could stay out a bit longer.

"I appreciate everything you've shared with me. I'm hoping you'll let me share something with you."

She nodded vigorously. "Anything."

"It requires a change of location," I said, dangling the words before her to see if she'd take the bait. Did I pass the test? "I'd like to introduce you to my wife."

Hesitation clouded her eyes, but I knew her type. She'd do anything to ease my pain. If that means coming with me to visit my wife's gravesite, so be it. She looked at her watch. She must have decided that she had a few minutes to spare, though, because she raised her head and nodded.

"Sure. Why not?"

And that is how my mother's fate was sealed.

CHAPTER 24

Amelia

Iowa City, 2024

I FLIP PAST THE rest of the chapter of Bridget's copy of *Beyond the Glass*, not wanting to remember the gruesome details of the crime. But there's no way to erase the memory of the way Gerald's face looked as he was telling me the story. The glee in his eyes, the pride. It reminded me of a father showing pictures of his baby, expecting the audience to respond with admiration.

A new father.

A baby.

The thought reminds me of something. In 2005, Shapiro abducted a woman named Susan Hodges. Originally, he planned to lock her in the basement for a week or so, long enough to give her hope that she would survive before he ended her life. But he had second thoughts. Because he found a kindred spirit in Susan. She had lost a sister when she was very young. The little girl drowned on a trip to the beach, and Susan had never quite gotten over it. He told me how he regretted his brother's death, wondering if the boy could have been the one to understand him. In Susan, Gerald saw a reflection of his own pain.

They got married and lived together for two years, long enough for Susan to get pregnant and have a baby. She gave birth to a baby boy, Simon, and it was difficult for Shapiro during that period of time. He wasn't terribly interested in children, and his own son was no exception. He didn't feel things like other fathers did. He was gone a lot, driving across the country, delivering goods to big box stores. One day he returned home to Susan, and she told him that he'd missed Simon's first steps. Gerald felt nothing. He then saw that Susan and the kid would be better off without him, so he left and never went back.

Simon Shapiro.

If anyone had reason to carry on his father's legacy, it's him.

I grab my phone and google him. A picture of an elderly man pops up. But Simon wouldn't be old now, he'd only be about 20. I google him again and add Gerald to the search terms. There are multiple links to my book, which chronicles Gerald's brief experience of being a father. I scroll past these and find a graduate thesis on psychopathy and genetics from a few years ago. It was written by Cynthia Mason, a student at the University of Chicago.

In the study, she interviewed the offspring of ten serial killers, and Simon was one of them. I scroll through the paper, looking for any mention of him. Twenty pages into the paper, she describes her meeting with Simon Shapiro. The questions delve into his upbringing, and Simon says that Gerald left his mother when he was extremely young. In the paper, Simon laments the fact he only got to know his father through newspaper clippings and a book—my book—in fact.

Mason said she used a Rorschach test to determine if Simon's responses deviated from the norm. During the testing, Simon revealed a tendency toward violence, more so than any of the other participants. A picture that looked like a cloud became a puddle of blood. A picture that looked like a moth became the face of the devil. Mason allows for the possibility that Simon was making up his responses to seem as though he were thoroughly affected by his relation to Gerald, but she emphasizes that he seemed natural as they went through the cards. Ultimately, Mason came to the conclusion that Simon did reflect a thought process like his father's, but she doubted he'd ever act on them. There's a door between thoughts and action, and she's almost sure he would never cross that threshold.

But what if she's wrong?

What if that's exactly what he's doing, reenacting his father's kills to feel closer to the man who should have raised him?

Maybe all he wants is for Gerald to notice him.

CHAPTER

25

Gabby

Iowa City, 2024

Friday night.
 Time to go to my dad's apartment.
 I sit on the couch by the front window, watching for his car. I've got my laptop on, scrolling through my social media. Everyone is talking about Bridget, wondering where she could be. There's a rumor that she ran off with the lead singer of her favorite band, Who Killed My Sea Monkeys. I guess she'd commented on one of his posts the night before, and he actually went and liked a bunch of her posts. Such bullshit.
 My dad pulls up in the Honda CRV he bought with my mother a year before he cheated; he'd gotten that car, and she'd bought a new one. I wish she'd find a new boyfriend.

I grab my bag and walk outside so my mom doesn't have to deal with him. He gets halfway out of his car and then sees that I'm already coming out to meet him.

"Ready?" he asks tersely. He was probably stressed about the possibility of seeing my mom. He glances toward the front door with apprehension.

I nod and climb into the SUV.

My father's irritation seems to dissipate when we pull out of the driveway and start heading to his apartment. He turns on the radio and twists the dial, rejecting a talk radio show and the country station.

"Yea or nay?" he asks when he settles on a classic rock station. The sound of Aerosmith fills the car. This is our little game, switching the station until we find a song that the other one likes. I'm not really in the mood for classic rock. I'm not really in the mood for anything, to be honest. I can't get Bridget Mahoney out of my head, and the peppy song about love in an elevator doesn't mesh with my thoughts.

"Can we just turn the radio off?" I ask.

"Sure," he says, glancing at me. "What's up?"

I think of the picture of the girl in *Beyond the Glass* with the spike through her head, red Sharpie blood cascading down the page. The girl's doodled face turns into Bridget's, and I can't stand it anymore. I wish I never read my mom's stupid book. But I can't complain. She warned me. I should have listened.

"I've been thinking about Bridget," I say, and his brow knits in concern.

"Were you two friends?"

Why would he ask me this? He knows we weren't. Most of my friends I've known since kindergarten, and they've either spent the night or invited me to their birthday parties. Although, I suppose, he hasn't kept close tabs on me since he moved out.

"Not really," I say, thinking about the fact that she's hot for my boyfriend. "Did you know her?"

"Not really," he echoes, but I detect something in his voice, a slight raise of inflection that usually means he isn't being completely honest. "She was in my class."

The rest of the ride is uneventful. Julia's car is there when we pull into the parking lot. She usually has yoga on Fridays, but she hasn't been going much lately. She just kind of hangs around the apartment and watches reality TV. I feel bad for her, actually, like she just gave up her whole life when she got together with my dad.

I lug my duffel bag into the apartment building, up the stairs, and down to the hall, where my dad holds the door for me. Everything looks as it always does. The living room is tidy and cozy as usual, with a quilt, made by Julia, laid over the back of the couch. A couple of craft magazines are arranged on the coffee table, along with a stack of library books.

"Will you be okay if I run a little errand?" my dad asks. "I've gotta take these books back to the library. Julia forgot, so I promised her I'd drop them off."

I eye the stack of books. The newest Karin Slaughter, a couple of Stephen Kings, and a copy of *What to Expect When You're Expecting*. My father follows my gaze, and he freezes.

"Damn it," he says. "I wanted to tell you myself."

Inside I am hollow. I'm sure many emotions will come seeping out of me as soon as I process this turn of events, but right now I'm in shock. It isn't real. It can't be real.

"But you're so . . . old," I say, followed by, "Sorry."

"I was hoping this would be something for us to look forward to. A new hope."

"Gabby," a voice comes from the kitchen. "I'm so glad you're here! I was hoping you'd make cookies with me."

I give a pointed look to my father, but he just shrugs and makes a kind of "I'm sorry" face before heading out the door. Pasting a cordial smile on my face, I drop my duffel bag in the hallway and head to the kitchen, where Julia is waiting for me, dressed in a festive Christmas apron, holding a wooden spoon.

"I didn't know what kind of cookies you liked, so I got a little of everything." Instead of the regular ingredients—eggs, sugar, flour—a variety of ready-made packages of cookie dough are scattered over the counter. Chocolate chip, snickerdoodle, and sugar cookies. She picks up the sugar cookies with Christmas tree designs on them. "These?"

"Whatever," I tell her. "I'm good with anything."

"Let's make them all, then," she exclaims. "I'm dying of hunger."

She rubs her tummy and must catch me looking at her strangely because she grabs my hand and says, "Isn't it exciting? You'll have a brother or sister at this time next year!"

It's suddenly a lot harder to keep the pleasant expression on my face. "Yeah, it's . . . something."

Her brow knits with concern. "Oh, honey, don't worry. We won't forget about you. In fact, I was hoping you'd come shopping with me to add things to my gift registry for the baby shower. I want you to be part of everything."

I can't help it; I suddenly remember meeting her for the first time. It was my freshman year, and I went to my dad's classroom after the last bell. There they were, the two of them. He was standing very close to her, considering she was his student teacher and a good twenty years younger than him. I got a very bad feeling. Things hadn't been good with my parents for a while, and I got a premonition that Julia was going to ruin everything.

I was right.

CHAPTER

26

Amelia

Iowa City, 2024

Simon, Simon.
Where is Simon now?
I remember Gerald talking about his son, the haunted look on his face as he described being a father. He couldn't control how he acted, how he tortured the young boy. Could he have damaged Simon in some way that twisted him irreparably? Enough that he'd follow in his father's footsteps and act out in the same way?

I'm sitting on my living room couch, drinking a glass of wine. As I sip, I look for Simon's current whereabouts. But he's like an Internet ghost. It seems like he's completely boycotting social media. If I weren't considering him as a suspect in the Bridget Mahoney kidnapping, I might even hire him to help clean up my own online profile. Then maybe I wouldn't get such psychotic fan mail.

I sit back and stare at the screen blankly, trying to figure out what to do next. I feel helpless here without Isaac. I try to get back in the mindset of solving puzzles that I was in when I interviewed Gerald Shapiro. I have to be curious. Anything could be a clue.

Wandering to the kitchen to refill my glass of wine, I mentally rehash what I've learned about Gerald that might lead me to his son. Maybe there's a family name that Simon would have adopted. His mother's maiden name? Hodges? I type in Simon Hodges, which seems like an awkward combination. Sure enough, there's nothing.

What about his middle name? That seems like a promising lead, but hell if I remember Simon's middle name. It might be in my book, though. I grab Bridget's copy of it and flip through the pages, looking for the chapter when Simon is born. Finally I find the section about his birth and sure enough, there's Simon's full name: Simon Russell Shapiro.

I plug the name into Google and get a few dozen hits. They're mostly on gaming websites, which announce the winners of various games like League of Legends, stuff like that. There's his Linked In profile, which has him working at a comic and game store for the past couple of years. Bingo. Using that information to track down his actual address in the white pages, I copy it down and plot my invasion.

Of course I'll have to take Isaac with me. If Simon's dangerous, I shouldn't be knocking on his door without any backup. I'm scared, but I'm also hopeful. The last time

I checked on Simon was when I was doing edits on *Beyond the Glass* five years ago, when he was about fifteen. I wonder what he looks like now. If he has his father's cold, dead eyes. Maybe he escaped the family curse.

I hope so.

CHAPTER

27

Gabby

Iowa City, 2024

When Julia goes to take a nap, I am left to my own devices. I wander around the apartment, trying to envision a baby there. I always wished for a little brother or sister, but this is not the way I pictured it—an addition to a family that already feels alien to me. My father barely spends time with me at all. Having a baby will only weaken the bond we have at the moment.

When I take my duffel bag to the guest room, I am taken aback. A whole wall is lined with baby paraphernalia. There are packages of diapers stacked into a precarious tower. Target bags full of things like pacifiers, tiny little nail clippers, and something that I think is used to suck boogers out of the kid's nose. The centerpiece of the mountain of baby stuff is a giant brown box with a picture of a crib on it.

Where are they going to put that crib? There's no room, considering the queen size bed on the opposite wall. I plop onto the bed, lean back, and cover my face with my arm. I'm not going to cry, I tell myself. It's not my room. They are free to decorate it however they want. But if they replace the bed with the crib, where am I supposed to sleep—the couch?

After a few minutes of feeling good and sorry for myself, I force myself to stand up and wander back into the living room. I turn on the TV to feel less lonely. There's a show with talking puppets on. Switching through the channels, I look for something to take my mind off what's going on in real life.

I stop changing channels when I come upon a news program. Leaning forward, I turn the volume up. In the upper right-hand corner, there's a picture of Bridget Mahoney. A phone number scrolls at the bottom of the screen, along with encouragement for anyone to come forward if they have any information. The reporter starts talking about the recent murders and how the Mahoney case is a race against time. My heart starts to pound hard, and I have a difficult time breathing. Unable to listen to any more, I turn off the TV and drop the remote control on the ground. I close my eyes and picture that black truck and Bridget kicking and screaming for help. I saw on a TV show once that said, after twenty-four hours, a victim's chances of survival go down substantially. We're getting close.

I need something to distract me, and the television obviously isn't doing the trick. I pick up a fashion magazine and look at ridiculous outfits that no one would ever wear outside. Frustrated, I throw the magazine back on the pile, and something catches my eye. It's a slender book with a red and white cover. When I uncover it, I realize it's the 2023 yearbook from my school. I find it strange that my father would keep a copy of it. Normally, he hides from the camera when the yearbook committee comes around. He says he already knows what he looks like, so he doesn't need a book to commemorate each and every year. The books are expensive, and if he bought one for every year, it would certainly add up.

I pick it up and open the cover, not sure what to expect. Who would sign a yearbook for my father? Whereas the front page is usually cluttered with notes like, "See you next year!" and "Have a great summer," this one is blank. There's no name on the inside, so I flip through the pages, looking for a clue of who this belongs to and why my father would have it.

There are several pages that are dog-eared, so I turn to the first one. There are pictures of the girls' volleyball team, candid shots of kids in the cafeteria, and a scene that looks like it's from inside the school library. I squint my eyes, trying to make out the people in the picture. In the foreground, Ms. Benning, the librarian, is shelving books. Behind her, there are a couple of kids on computers. And in the corner, a girl curves into her chair, cradling a book.

Bridget.

Why is this page dog-eared? Quickly, I turn the pages until I get to the next dog-eared one. In this one, six rows of kids in my grade are staring back at me, their names featured below each picture. Third row, sixth from the left, is Bridget Mahoney. Not that I can see her face well, because of the Sharpie marker scribbled over her face.

I feel sick to my stomach, dropping the yearbook on the carpet. I barely make it to the bathroom before heaving my guts up. It's a long time before the sickness subsides. When I've recovered, I flush the toilet and stand up and look at myself in the mirror.

What I see there is my father's face. While people who read my mom's book always say I look like her, the people at school who know my dad say I look just like him, with high cheekbones and arched eyebrows. My eyes are the same as his, bright blue. Whereas my father's going gray, I have the same dark brown tresses that he had when he was young. It's not just looks I got from my father, either. All my life he'd tell me stories—whenever we traveled somewhere new, he told me about famous people who'd lived and worked there. It's what makes him such a good teacher. He makes things interesting.

What story is behind this yearbook? What story will he tell?

I'm not ready to confront him about it, so I grab the yearbook and stick it in my bag with seconds to spare before he opens the front door.

"I got Chinese," he announces cheerfully.

My appetite is nonexistent. My stomach feels like it's eating itself, but I pretend to be happy about the surprise meal. "Yum."

After setting the white cartons of lo mein and kung pao chicken on the small dining room table, he grabs plates from the kitchen, and we sit together, watching the news, barely talking. After we've finished, my dad picks up the messenger bag that he uses to transport student papers to and from school.

"Are you going somewhere?" I ask.

"I just need to go to school to get some grading done. Shouldn't be too long."

I nod and pick at a single grain of rice that has fallen on the table.

It seems strange that my father would want to go to the school to grade papers. Normally he just does it on the couch with some smooth jazz playing. Maybe he wants to get away from Julia, who is fluttering around the apartment with a rag, dusting. The nesting period has already started, I guess.

I go to bed early, before he gets home. I wrap myself in two quilts and pull them up over my head, acutely aware of the crib that is sitting a few feet away, waiting to be assembled.

CHAPTER

28

The Kidnapper

Homestead, 2024

RENEE KEEPS CALLING, but I don't pick up the phone. She'll be livid that I haven't followed her directions to kill the girl yet.

I won't until I figure out what I'm going to do.

After I cleaned the girl up, I locked her back downstairs, although I didn't tie her up too tight. I didn't want her to soil her pants again, so I put a bucket down there too. There's no way for her to get out. Out of all the girls who have briefly spent time in my basement, no one has ever escaped. My idea is to hold her for ransom, get some money out of her parents. I already threw her phone away, dumped it in the river on my way out of town, but I know who she is from the news broadcasts that have been on the TV nonstop. I was able to find the rest online.

Bridget Mahoney of 1836 Scott Boulevard.

Daughter of Rachel and Mark Mahoney.

I even find phone numbers.

I use a website to create a fake phone number to contact Bridget's parents with. Using my laptop, I send a message using a VPN that routes my call from Indonesia. I choose the mother's cell because I figure she's the one who will drive this situation forward with her love for her daughter, her desperation to see her come home. I can't decide how much to ask for, but I finally choose to be realistic.

$50K and I'll give your daughter back.

Fifty thousand isn't that much in the grand scheme of things, but it's more likely that the Mahoneys will have access to that amount. It'll be enough to pay for a nice honeymoon for me and Renee, and the rest can be socked away for a rainy day . . . or more likely, a day we have to run. And there's no way the Mahoneys are seeing Bridget again. As soon as I get that cash, she will be making friends with the fishes.

Until then, I need to keep her alive.

I sigh and slap my knees, pushing myself to my feet. I don't really have much in this place for her to eat, but I think I've got some crackers somewhere. Probably stale as hell, but it's not like she'll be complaining. I grab a glass of water, too, then pull on my mask before I head down to the basement. The girl is huddled up with her knees against her chest, her wrists tied to a water pipe.

She scowls.

Anger stirs up inside me. I don't have to be doing all this, helping her up to the bathroom, rinsing her off, bringing her food like she's the goddamn queen of England. None of the others got that kind of treatment.

I set the plate of food and glass down next to her.

She splays her fingers around the pipe. "How'm I supposed to eat—with my feet?"

With a jerk, she kicks out and sends the glass flying, spilling water everywhere.

I slap her. Hard.

Her face remains turned away for a few moments, and when she looks back, I expect her to be crying. But there is a hard, cold hate in her eyes. She stares at me so long that I start to get itchy to hit her again, teach her who's boss.

I don't.

Instead, I meet her stare with one of my own—the kind my father used to give me when I back-talked him or stole one of his cigarettes. The kind that means business, the life or death kinda business.

"I know you didn't mean to take me," she says, and that surprises me.

"What do you mean?"

"I heard you shout something earlier. You said you had 'a girl,' not 'the girl.' Who were you supposed to take?" Her eyes narrow to slits. "I know who you meant to take. Gabby. She's the only other girl who was there. What did you want with her?"

Before I even realize what I'm doing, I've got her by the hair, and she's screaming. My heart is pounding so fast, I can feel it in my throat. How does this girl know I was trying to take Amelia's girl? There's no way she's getting out of this now. I make myself let go of her and stand up, pacing, trying to figure out what to do next.

"If you didn't mean to take me, just give me back. You're wearing a mask. I don't know what you look like. I won't tell anyone. I swear."

I've heard this before and never believed any woman who promised silence. There's no reason for me to start buying this girl's story, no matter how much I might want to be through with this whole mess.

"No, you won't," I say.

On the way upstairs, I flip off the light, leaving her in the dark.

CHAPTER

29

Amelia

Iowa City, 2024

Isaac meets me at Freshly Ground—the coffee shop where Bridget was last seen. It's on the ground floor of a now-crumbling brick building off East 23rd Street. If you didn't know better, you'd think you were in a nightclub.

Booths line the walls of the homey little cafe, with black-and-white posters of models like Kate Moss and Johnny Depp stretched over the windows. It is dark, incredibly so. There's no overhead lighting, only little lamps at each table to illuminate the menus listing all manner of lattes and espressos. A cute little pink-haired pixie with a labret piercing comes around to take us to our seat.

"This might be weird," I say, "but can you seat us where Bridget Mahoney was sitting yesterday?"

She frowns. "Why would you wanna know that?"

Isaac flashes his badge and says, "We're tracing her last whereabouts."

The girl doesn't look very happy, but she points us to a booth in the back of the room.

Once seated, I lean down to look beneath the booth, not really sure what I'm looking for. It's not like she would have left anything behind. They probably swept and mopped when they closed last night. No, the only thing under the booth are wads of chewed up gum in every color of the rainbow.

Someone clears their throat.

The girl with the labret piercing is back to take our order. I straighten up in time to smile politely at the girl.

"Can you tell me anything about Bridget Mahoney?" I ask.

"I'm sorry. I've told everything I could think of to the police," she says. "Can I get you something to drink? Coffee? Soda?"

I bury my nose in the menu.

"Do you know what Bridget ordered when she was here?"

The girl shifts uncomfortably on her feet. "Um, no. I didn't take her order."

"Did you notice anyone around who could have been watching her?" Isaac asks, patting his shirt pocket, looking for a pen and pad of paper.

She stands with her head cocked, thinking.

"Actually, there was a man in here before her. He was hanging around, looking like he was waiting for someone. I didn't think anything of it."

Isaac clicked his pen and asked, "What did he look like?"

She shrugged. "I don't know. He was white. Brown hair. I don't know what color his eyes were. He just looked like a normal guy."

"There was nothing unusual about him?"

"Hmmmm..."

Both Isaac and I are on the edge of our seats. There must be something, anything she can remember about him. His clothes. A watch. A wallet. Something.

She says, "Well, he didn't order anything. He was just sitting in the back, flipping through this weird red-and-black book."

I think about my daughter sitting here, in the same room with him, and my blood runs cold. What if he was watching her, biding his time before she left and he could attack her? Only poor Bridget came out instead.

The waitress looks at us in concern. "Do you think he had something to do with her disappearance?" She twists her hands together. "Maybe it was him. Maybe it was him and we just let him go." Her voice is panicky.

"Look, there's nothing you could do," Isaac reassures her. "Don't worry about it."

I wait until we get outside to speak. "A red-and-black book? What if it was—"

Isaac nods grimly. "*Beyond the Glass.*"

"It can't be a coincidence," I say.

I want him to disagree with me, tell me I'm being silly, jumping to conclusions.

But he doesn't.

"I think you're right," he finally replies. "I think he may have been after Gabby."

CHAPTER

30

Beyond the Glass

(A. Child, 2019, pp. 62–64)

Gerald was a celebrity—in his own mind, of course—but he did have fans popping up in Reddit threads and on true crime blogs as the years went on. People speculated about where he was, what he was doing. They had fights about whether certain murders were committed by him. After he was convicted, a fan went to the extreme and sent a letter to the media, saying that he was going to kill someone to pledge his loyalty to Gerald.

His name was Jeremy Baker, and he'd had a troubled childhood. From elementary school and onward, he'd been teased about his weight and the fact that his mother had died when he was young. You'd think that such a person would appeal to the side of Gerald who was also motherless, but Gerald later said he was weak and could not relate to him.

The teen began posting videos declaring his love for Gerald Shapiro. He had Gerald's name tattooed on his calf. He gathered items like knives and rope and put them in a "kill kit." He was like a teenage girl gushing about her favorite band. He created a top ten list of his favorite kills, and his YouTube went viral, though he didn't share any identifying information for authorities to come after him. He used a VPN to post his content, so he couldn't be tracked down. Eventually, after hundreds of complaints, YouTube shut down his channel for good.

Without his platform, Jeremy was lost. He kept making videos, but he had nowhere to post them, no words of support from like-minded peers. He sank deeper into depression, and on his Twitter account, he said he no longer had a reason to live. He explained in great detail the sacrifice he was about to make in Gerald's honor.

Jeremy had been lusting after a girl ahead of him in school, Laura Benson, sending creepy texts about them being soulmates. She avoided him at all costs, but one afternoon Jeremy showed up on her doorstep with a gun and shot her right there, then shot himself. A letter he left behind pledged that the girl and he would be waiting for Gerald in hell, and they would all be together, forever.

A nonprofit organization started a media campaign to caution people who saw any of the warning signs that Baker exhibited. *When in doubt, call them out.* They set up a tip line for people to call if they saw any similar threats online.

The tip line is still in use today. See the appendix for the number and guidelines for reporting potential violent acts. The tip line has saved multiple lives, and it has the potential of saving many more.

If you see someone exhibiting violence online, please call the number.

Better safe than sorry.

CHAPTER

31

Gabby

Iowa City, 2024

Easton rarely visits my dad's apartment ever since he once walked in on Julia and my father getting it on. I don't blame him. I prefer to stay in the guest room when Julia's home because, no matter how comfortable she tries to make me, I feel like a stranger in a strange world.

But Julia has gone to prenatal yoga and my father has gone to the gym. They'll take a couple of hours. They usually like to go to brunch after their workouts and then sometimes shopping. So when Easton comes over, he's relieved to see they aren't there.

He stands in the doorway of the spare room, peering inside. "Well, fuck."

"Precisely," I say. "It's a babyland hellscape."

He has to move several packages of diapers to make room enough on the floor to sit. "So, what's this emergency?"

The yearbook is under my pillow. Half of me wants to put it back where my father can find it so he won't know I took it, but the other half needs to know what the fuck is going on. To show or not to show, that is the question. I want to ask my dad and realize he has a perfectly reasonable explanation. But what if he doesn't have one? What if he's involved with Bridget's disappearance somehow? What if this is the evidence that could send him to jail? I'm mad at him for leaving Mom for Julia and even more so about the baby, but that doesn't mean I want to see him in prison for the rest of his life. By showing Easton, this will become much bigger; it will become real. I have to remind myself, it's already real. I just don't know the truth.

When I withdraw the yearbook from my bag, Easton squints at it. "I thought we made fun of people who bought those. Fake memories. Carefully crafted to paint a rosier picture than what real high school is like."

"It isn't mine," I reply, barely more than a whisper.

"Then whose is it?"

Easton takes the book from me and starts flipping through it. He lands on the first dog-eared page and examines it.

"It belongs to Bridget Mahoney."

"What?" Easton looks up at me in surprise. "How did you get it?"

If I tell, I could lose my father forever.

But if I don't, I'll never know the truth.

It's hard to tell which is worse.

I swallow. "You can never tell anyone. I mean it. *No one.*"

Easton stares at me for a long moment. "You can trust me."

It's so hard to get the words out. "I got it from my father."

"That can't be right," Easton says, but I see a glimmer of doubt in his eyes.

He flips through the pages until he comes upon the picture of Bridget that's been scribbled out. He goes pale. "Why would . . . ?"

"I don't know!" I exclaim. "I don't know why he would do that. I was hoping you'd come up with a reasonable explanation for this, because I sure as hell can't."

Easton continues to peel the pages back, looking for some clue I might have missed. We discuss the lack of signatures in the book, how sad it was that she had no friends to write "See you next year" in her yearbook, but there's no one who would have a vendetta against Bridget.

After a while, we just sit there on the bed with the yearbook closed on the floor. It's too much for me to think about, too much for me to handle. Tears sting my eyes. Easton looks at me sympathetically and brushes my hair back from my face.

"I have something I need to tell you," he tells me.

At the moment, I can't think of anything worse than this. But I can't stop now. I've opened my eyes to see a possibility I never imagined. What's one more terrible thing?

"Um, you know how I stayed late last Wednesday to retake that bio test?"

I seem to remember him saying something about it, but I can't imagine what that could possibly have to do with this. "Yeah?"

He takes a deep breath, his blue eyes like the fathomless depths of a deep blue sea. I dread what's behind those eyes. I don't want him to tell me. But that's not how this works.

"I was done with my math test," he says, picking off a nonexistent piece of fuzz from his pants. "I went to my locker to get my bag, and I saw something."

My patience is at an all-time low. "What? What did you see?"

"I saw Bridget," he says, his voice so low it's hardly audible. "She was coming out of your dad's classroom. And she was crying."

I stare at him with wide eyes.

"That can't be true. You're lying, Easton."

Easton drops his head into his hands and says, his voice muffled through his fingers, "I'm sorry, Gabby. I wasn't going to tell you, but then Bridget disappeared and everyone was freaking out, and I just wanted to protect you."

I can't find a response. All I'm thinking about is Bridget's body buried in the woods or sunk in some nearby lake. My father isn't capable of something like that. He's the man who put SpongeBob Band-Aids on my wounds. He got me a glass of water when I couldn't sleep and would gently tuck me back into bed. I can't picture him making anyone cry, let alone kidnap them. This is all wrong.

"Protect me?" I demand. "Or protect you?"

"What do you mean?" Easton looks bewildered.

"I mean, it doesn't look great that Bridget disappeared and it turns out that you were dating her and she was keeping your picture secret. And you didn't tell anyone!"

"Gabby," he says, his voice low. "You know I didn't have anything to do with what happened to her. I was with you, for Christ's sake."

What he says is true. He couldn't have been involved. But if what he's saying is true, it means my father might be the culprit, which is inconceivable to me.

"Should we call the police then?" he asks, pulling his phone out of his pocket. He starts to dial. I stare at him as he hits 9 and then 1 and then—

"No!" I cry. "This is all a misunderstanding. If we tell, he might go to prison for a very long time or maybe even forever. We have to find out more before we do that. I mean, this isn't really incriminating evidence. We need a bloody knife or a confession or something."

Easton raises one eyebrow, the one he always raises when he plays devil's advocate. "Yeah, but if we don't tell the police, we are responsible for any more girls that go missing. Do you want that?"

I picture the women in *Beyond the Glass*, the disgusting collages Gerald Shapiro made using their pictures. There's no way my dad could hurt people like that.

Could he?

"Give it a week," I say desperately.

"Bridget could be dead by then," he replies. "I'm sorry, I can't do this."

I watch him as he gets up and walks out the door, leaving me with the yearbook of a kidnapped and possibly dead girl. The only way I'm going to save my father is by figuring out who the real culprit is. And fast.

CHAPTER

32

Amelia

Iowa City, 2024

By the time we get back from the coffee shop, it's late. Since Gabby's at her father's, I decide to just order pizza while Isaac and I relax. I pour us each a glass of wine and set them on the coffee table, along with some veggies and hummus for us to snack on until the pizza gets here. Isaac falls onto the couch, looking exhausted, and I do the same.

When the pizza comes, I get out the paper plates and serve myself a big slice of Canadian bacon and pineapple, a combination that Jack rarely ever let me get. I half-heartedly flip through the channels and stop on the news.

"Tonight is the second night that Bridget Mahoney has been missing," announces a woman with a neat bob and a bright blue jacket. Bridget's school picture flashes on screen, her features reminding me again of how much she looks like my own daughter. I can't dismiss the feeling that Bridget had just been there, the wrong time and place. The only consolation I have is that Gabby is safe at Jack's house right now.

"You look like you need some more wine," Isaac says, and he picks up the wine bottle.

I cover my glass with my hand, feeling a bit woozy from the wine I drank earlier in the afternoon. "I'm good."

I watch him for a long moment, marveling that we're back together again, after years of not even talking. Since Gerald was put in jail. And now there's another monster on the loose. The two of us only seem to come together when there's danger on the horizon.

He leans over and before I know it, our mouths are pressed together. At first, I am surprised, but then I let myself melt into his arms. It's been so long. Since Jack, even. I've spent the past few years hiding in our house, researching and writing and revising. Lather, rinse, repeat. I haven't even had a date since our divorce.

But now I'm making up for all that. As he runs his hands through my hair, my heart feels like it's going to beat right out of my chest. For just a moment, I am almost able to forget there's a missing girl out there and that it might be my fault.

Isaac pulls away.

"Do you know how long I've been waiting to do that?" he asks.

"Not nearly as long as me," I say, and it's the truth.

Things had gone bad with me and Jack far before the end, and I had fantasized about this many, many times. For a brief moment I'm able to let go of the horror of Bridget's kidnapping and just be in the moment with him. Afterwards, we fall asleep on the couch like that, and I feel safe for the first time in such a long time.

CHAPTER 33

Beyond the Glass

(A. Child, 2019, pp. 79–82)

Psychopaths tend to be loners in their dark profession, but every once in a while, they find a kindred spirit along the way. There is a certain vibe they give off, Gerald told me.

> It's kind of like love at first sight, I guess, but that's a bad analogy. It's more like . . . respect at first sight. We recognize each others' games, I guess, the little comments we sneak into conversations to demean the other person or the act of snowing another person, completely sucking up to them until they believe they're something real special and then you pull the rug out from under them and they fall, so hard.

It was when I was working at the auto parts factory. After my previous boss had met an unfortunate end, a new supervisor took his place. You know that saying about not focusing on your job too much because if you die, they'll replace you before you're in the ground? It was that kind of situation.

This new guy's name was Chris Daniels, and he was slick, let me tell you. A handshake like a death grip. When we met, I made a joke about hoping he lasted longer than the last guy, and the look he gave me— well, I saw myself in him. He looked me up and down, and my cover was completely blown. It's hard to explain, but he knew what I was, and I knew what he was.

At first, it was business as usual. But after a few weeks, Chris asked me to go get a couple of beers after work. We went to this sports bar where balding dads watched a little basketball before heading home to their pudgy wives and grubby children. I didn't drink much. I don't like to feel out of control, plus it makes me feel like my father, someone I did not care to emulate in the slightest.

Chris only had a drink or two as well before suggesting we go for a walk. I thought it was a strange question, but I was curious so I said yes. I figured if he was going to try to hurt me, I could probably overpower him. He drove us to a park on the bad side of town. After dark, you'd have to be real crazy to go there. Lucky for Chris, I was real crazy. In the order of the food chain, I was at the top.

He led me down a trail, where he showed me a place in the woods where you could see whoever was coming down the path if you crouched down. I joined him, just wanting to see where things led. Sure enough, a young woman jogged by, headphones on. Not the safest way to go for a run.

Before I knew it, Chris had leapt out of the bushes and was running after the girl. He must have been a runner himself because he closed the distance between them in an instant. He jumped on her, bringing her down, and smashed her face into the ground. Then he looked up at me with the oddest expression. Like he was a dog bringing me a dead bird. He was just waiting for me to react, either in disgust or as if I were grateful.

He got nothing. I left him there, to his own devices.

CHAPTER 34

The Kidnapper

Homestead, 2024

It takes the Mahoneys thirty-two minutes to respond to my message.

The thought that they may have contacted the police crosses my mind, but the threat to their daughter's safety makes me reasonably sure that they're just figuring out where they're going to get that kind of cash.

I recline in my chair watching the TV with the sound off. The girl's school picture flickers on and off the screen, along with a number to call if anyone has any information. Nothing new, no license plate, no identifying information about me, only the tip about the black pickup truck seen in the parking lot. I'm feeling okay. I'm feeling safe.

Finally, a new email pops up in my fake account. It's a text from the mom's cell phone number: Can you give us a few days, please?

Just as I thought. They need time to scrape together that kind of money. Most people I know wouldn't be able to walk into their bank and withdraw $50,000. It would require withdrawing money from investments, retirement accounts. The request doesn't surprise me, but I'd be lying if it doesn't make me feel a little nervous. The longer I hold on to this kid, the higher the chances the authorities will find something I left behind, although I'm fairly sure I left no trace. But the little things start niggling at me, like I was wearing fairly distinctive boots at the time, and it was snowing. I left Iowa City so quickly, not even checking to see if I left prints in the mud or gravel, a perfect mold of the bottom of my old Timberlands.

I eye them, neatly positioned on the rug by the door. I hate to get rid of them, had them since high school, but I've gotta do it if I want to destroy any evidence. Not that it will help until I get rid of the girl, too. The thought of keeping her around a couple more days makes me antsy as hell.

But then I think of what that money can do. Fix up the house real nice for Renee. She deserves to have a nice home to spend the rest of her life in. She works so hard, she needs someone to take care of her for once, instead of the other way around. I could paint the walls a nice, warm color, like the butter yellow of the sundress she was wearing when I first met her. Or green, like her eyes. I'll build her bookshelves from wall to wall. Maybe I could even afford to rebuild that porch out front. Right now it's falling apart. Yeah. I can wait a couple days.

I send a message to say they've got twenty-four hours, starting right now, to get that money into my account or it's the end of their daughter. They get right back to me, thanking me, promising they'll get the money ASAP. It makes me wonder what I would do in that situation, if Renee and I had a daughter of our own. Right away, I push the thought aside. You can't afford to think that way in my line of work.

CHAPTER

35

Beyond the Glass

(A. Child, 2019, pp. 79–82)

After weeks of interviewing Gerald about the terrible things that happened to him, as well as the horror he wreaked on other people, I decided to change course and investigate his childhood. I was obsessed with the question of whether Gerald was born bad or whether he evolved to be that way. I interviewed his teachers to see what he was like, to see if he'd always been a problem.

I went back as far as kindergarten, speaking with his elementary school teachers. I was afraid that they wouldn't remember him, as it had been so long ago, but his kindergarten teacher Mrs. Woods recalled him in almost perfect detail.

"He was precocious, that was for sure. By that time his mother had left, so it was his father who dropped him off and picked him up from school. Well, it started out that way, but more often his babysitter would come to get him in the afternoon."

"So, what was he like?"

"He was creative," Mrs. Woods said. "I understand that his art took a bit of a macabre turn later on, but when he was in my classroom, he drew pictures of the normal things, the sun, trees, his family."

"What did the pictures of his family look like?"

"They were normal except when he explained it to me, it seems the woman in the picture was his babysitter. There was one curiosity. He drew the family standing on a hill, but beneath the hill was another stick figure, lying horizontally across the bottom."

It hit me before she could even say it. "His brother."

"Yes, it was his younger brother, Noah."

"Did he explain it to you?"

"I'll never forget it. He said, 'Noah hates the water.' I'd gotten a heads-up from the principal before he started school that he had lost his brother when he was very little. It made sense that he would draw his brother that way. I thought it indicated that he was still very much mourning his sibling. I didn't hear the circumstances until after he was out of my class. The chill that went through me when I heard it—It's like nothing I'd felt before. But I felt that way again, when I heard that Gerald was arrested for all those murders later on."

All of Gerald's teachers had a similar story. He was bright, but there was something off about him that came through in his schoolwork. His English teacher called home to talk about a disturbing short story in which he shot his mother in the head. His art teacher said he took pictures of roadkill and sometimes put them in weird positions. He told his math teacher he was going to skin him and make him into a coat.

When I asked his high school teachers if they were afraid of him at one time or another, 100% of them said yes. Same for his boss at the grocery store where he worked when he was sixteen. Same for the neighbors that lived near him growing up. They all had that in common.

Fear.

So when we talk about whether Gerald's actions were precipitated by nature or nurture, we have to consider that it might not be an either-or proposition. He drew pictures of the sun and flowers, but he also drew a picture of the brother he drowned at a very young age. Maybe it was jealousy that drove him to those actions or maybe it was a sick urge to see what would happen if he deprived his brother of oxygen; perhaps it was a combination of the two, but the outcome is the same. Death. He sought to destroy everything beautiful and innocent that crossed his path.

That is what we call a monster.

CHAPTER 36

Amelia

Iowa City, 2024

Isaac takes the wheel, and we travel I-80 West. It's a route I've driven many times, but this somehow seems different. It isn't actually that far from Iowa City to Newton, where Gerald Shapiro is housed, but the road ahead seems to stretch on forever.

"You should try to get some rest," Isaac tells me.

"I don't want to," I reply.

I feel a bit like a child going on a dreaded vacation with the family. I keep seeing Bridget's face and wondering what's happening to her right now. Unfortunately, I can picture what's going on. After all, I was the one who interviewed the original Catfish Killer.

I know what he's like.

Who's to say this new bastard won't do the same depraved things as his predecessor?

Instead, I turn over what happened with Isaac in my mind. It seemed like such a great idea at the time, to open myself emotionally and physically. Both of us were looking for something to make us feel less helpless. But I can't get it out of my head that it was wrong somehow, like I'm not ready. It's not that I still have hope of me getting back together with Jack, but jumping into a relationship with Isaac seems like a bad idea.

"What's wrong?" Isaac asks, glancing at me. "Are you having regrets?"

It seems as though he's read my mind. It's somehow both reassuring and unsettling.

"Any regrets I might harbor have nothing to do with you," I say, tilting my head back on the headrest. The lack of sleep has begun weighing on me, and my eyelids droop as we drive past endless corn and soybean fields. "Do you regret it?"

He takes a moment in answering. "Any regrets I have are the amount of time we wasted not being together. You don't know how much I've missed you since—"

"Since the last time," I finish his sentence.

Why is it that we only get together when the world is falling apart?

"You could have called when you heard about the divorce. But you didn't," I say.

He flicks on his turn signal and passes a minivan being driven by an elderly woman whose hair is the bright blue of a robin's egg. "I didn't know if you were ready. It was safer to wait until you reached out. And I wasn't sure you ever would."

I turn my head to look at him. "And all this time, you've just been pining away for me? Do you take me for a fool?"

"Of course not," he says, to both questions, I think. "Everyone thinks they're getting the fairy tale when they're starting out," he goes on. "It just took you longer to figure it out."

I look at him curiously.

I wonder what his former wife is like. I saw her at a gas station once. She was the complete opposite of me, with long blonde hair and a heart-shaped face. I wonder if he still thinks about her. It seems odd that we've known each other so long, and yet it seems like, in a way, we don't know each other at all.

"Isaac, are you happy?" I ask.

Perhaps it is a strange question to ask in these circumstances, but in another way, it seems like the only thing that matters.

"I don't believe in happy," he replies. I must be frowning because he rushes on to explain himself. "I mean, I suppose someone can feel happy, but it's not something you can be long term. I would say mostly I'm content. I have the basic necessities, and I have my work. That's more than a lot of people have. And I must be satisfied with that."

I squint at him, trying to determine if he's just full of shit and trying to evade the question. But he looks genuine, his eyes clear and wide.

"What about you? Are you happy?"

I laugh softly. "You know I'm not. I mean, obviously." I gesture toward the light line on my ring finger that never seems to go away.

"Sometimes we cling to things that don't serve us anymore because we mistakenly believe that things will change.

When you know deep down that they won't." If he were lecturing me, I would let his words go in one ear and out the other, but he is gentle with his criticism, and I have to admit that he's right.

"Sometimes I worry about Gabby. I think that maybe we're harming her in some way, by not giving her the happily ever after."

He touches my hand.

"Of course you're not harming her," he says. "You're the best mom I know."

I think about how Gabby's doing, but I tell myself that she will be fine. Jack knows how to entertain her, and he's always complaining about how he never gets to see her. A girl's life is in my hands. My relationship with Gabby can sit on the back burner for a few days.

"How much longer?" I ask.

Isaac checks his smart watch. "About half an hour."

"What's the game plan?"

I'm hoping that he has a good one because nothing is really popping into my mind.

"Let me handle it," Isaac says. He pats his pocket, where I know he keeps his badge. Sometimes I forget he's a detective and that he does this all the time. For me, this is my whole world, finding this girl. None of us will be safe until we find the culprit. I drum my fingers on the center console, wishing he could go faster.

The sooner we find this bastard, the sooner it will all be over.

CHAPTER 37

Beyond the Glass

(A. Child, 2019, pp. 91–93)

If we are to posit the idea that psychopathy is an inherited trait, we must closely examine the traits of Gerald Shapiro's grandfathers on both sides. Psychopathy is akin to severe antisocial behavior, which was observed in his grandfather on his father's side.

Philip Shapiro was born into a middle-class family with the good luck to have an aunt as a benefactor who paid for his education as long as he stayed in line. He majored in finance, and he worked on Wall Street in the forties. The economy had just rebounded and was as healthy as ever, leading to a hefty paycheck, which Philip invested in stocks, the dividends of which paid for his and his wife's lavish lifestyle.

A man who lived his life transactionally, Philip provided the very best for his family, but he always expected the very best in return. Gerald's father, Tom, was enrolled in private school and, during his holidays, flew to Aspen to ski or Hawaii to surf. He was provided an impressive wardrobe, clothes for every occasion. He never lacked for presents on Christmas or his birthday.

Except for when he misbehaved.

Philip had been raised by the belt, and he continued that tradition in his family. He may have seemed suave and debonaire, but behind closed doors, he was a monster, wreaking havoc on his wife and children.

If his wife did anything he disapproved of, he would lock her in her room without food or drink, until she repented whatever it was that she had done. Sometimes it was spilling food on a new dress. Other times it was because she had the nerve to smile at another man.

When it came to Tom, Philip beat him according to his mood. He was described as pouring boiling water all over Tom's back, enough to raise the skin in unsightly boils. But he never hurt the child where teachers or acquaintances might see the bruises and sores. This was the key lesson Tom learned, growing up in that environment.

Philip Shapiro would say of Tom that he pissed away his future, drinking away any money he had, cheating on his wife, and neglecting his son. Frustrated by his son's inability to tackle life with the same vigor, Gerald's grandfather cut his Tom out of the will, effectively disinheriting him, leaving Gerald with a drunken father who had no capacity to care for a child.

So you see, the sins of their fathers carried on.

And Gerald was left holding the bag.

CHAPTER

38

Gabby

Iowa City, 2024

I NEED TO GET away from my father's apartment so I can think things through, but I have no one to take me back to my mom's house. I end up walking the two miles, wind whipping through my hair and frost nipping at my ears. Most of the streets have been plowed, so I don't have to wade through monstrous snowbanks, but I have to be careful about the patches of ice along the way. My backpack thumps against me as I walk along.

My mind won't stop racing. It's been working overtime ever since I found that damn yearbook. After Easton left, I put it back where I found it, just in case my father looks for it. I don't want him to know that I'm on to him.

No, no, no.

He's done nothing wrong. He just has one of his students' yearbooks. Maybe Bridget accidentally left it in his room and he picked it up and forgot he had it. There are a million reasonable explanations.

By the time I reach my house, my cheeks and nose are so red I look like a lobster. I notice the mail on the dining room table before I rush to the bathroom and run a hot bath. Luxuriating in the warmth of the water, I relax in it for about ten minutes before the guilt gets to me, and I know I have to get out and look for more clues as to where Bridget is. After draining the tub, I go to my room and pull on some cleanish jeans and a turtleneck sweater.

On my way to the kitchen to make myself a nice cup of tea, the mail on the dining room table catches my eye. One envelope in particular. It has no return address, but that's not the weird thing about it. On it, my name is written in red ink. My heart stops, and I pick up the envelope, stick my index finger into the flap and open it, giving myself a papercut.

"Shit," I exclaim and stick my finger into my mouth to suck off the blood. It's like pennies in my mouth.

I pull out the piece of paper that has been folded in thirds. It's a page from a book, it looks like, the left side all jagged like someone ripped it out hastily. I look at the title at the top of the page, and it says *Beyond the Glass*. Besides that, all the words on the paper have been colored over in black Sharpie, leaving only two words behind.

YOU'RE NEXT

I gasp and drop the letter on the floor, taking a step away from it as if it's a snake about to bite. Looking around, I feel like I'm being watched. Eyes everywhere. Whoever has taken Bridget has been here, in my house. Suddenly everywhere is a hiding spot. He could be in the pantry or waiting in the hallway. He could be behind the basement door, just waiting to pop out and grab me.

Grabbing a knife from the block on the kitchen counter, I wave it around, ready to attack whoever might come at me. I edge toward the kitchen door and yell hoarsely. "I've got a knife! Whoever you are, you'd better get the fuck out of here!"

I think about grabbing my cell phone to call 911 and then realize it's still at the police station, being tested for malware. And my mom never did install a landline when we moved in, though she meant to.

Just then, I hear metal scraping against concrete. Mike, our handyman, is shoveling the driveway. I grab the letter and run outside to ask him about it.

"Did you see who left this?" I ask breathlessly.

Mike examines the envelope. "No. I just brought it in, I didn't look at it. What is it? Is everything okay?"

I exhale. If he brought it in, that means the kidnapper isn't necessarily in the house. I just have to grab what I need and get the hell out of here.

"Yeah," I say, although I'm sure he can see right through me. "Everything's fine."

I go inside, close the door, and then rest against it for several minutes, breathing hard.

Finally, I catch my breath. When I've gotten a hold of myself, I step into my sneakers, pull on a jacket, and grab my backpack before heading out the door. My hair, still wet from the bath, freezes almost immediately into something like straw. The snow spills into my sockless shoes, probably freezing my toes, but I can't even feel it.

All I feel is terror.

When I ring the doorbell of our neighbor, Mrs. Doss answers the door in a housecoat, her hair in curlers. She takes one look at me and ushers me inside.

"Poor girl, what's happened?"

"Can I use your phone?" I pant.

She nods and holds the door open for me, guides me to sit down on the couch next to a coffee table with the phone on it. I pick up the receiver and dial my mom's number. It rings and rings and eventually goes to her voicemail. She must be at the prison, questioning Gerald.

Mrs. Doss hovers nearby, like she doesn't know what she should do. "Would you like some water, dear?" I nod, whatever, as long as she goes away while I figure this out. She disappears deeper in the house, and I hear the water running.

Where can I go? I'm still mad at Easton. I know he'd let me come over if I explain the letter, but he'll probably find some way to pin it on my father, even though that's ludicrous because why would he want to hurt me, even if he is a psycho kidnapper? Still, I don't want to go back to my father's apartment, either.

Mrs. Doss comes tottering back from the kitchen, a glass of water in her hands. They shake as he passes me the drink, and it reminds me of my grandfather, so fragile, so frail. And then it hits me. I can call my grandfather. Mom is not super close with him for some reason. Evidently, they had a falling out long ago, but I'm sure he'd take me in if he knew what was going on. I have his number written in my notebook because I made a list of people to call for a basketball fundraiser about a month ago. Shaking, I take the notebook out and thumb through it until I find the page with his number. I dial it slowly, deliberately.

The phone rings a couple of times, and I'm already wondering if there's anyone else I could call, but then he picks up.

"Hello?"

Will he even remember me?

"Hi, Grandpa," I say. "It's me, Gabby."

"Gabby! Good to hear from you. How are you?"

Mrs. Doss raises her eyebrows. I give her the thumbs up, and she graciously leaves the room to let me have a private conversation with my grandfather.

"To tell you the truth, I'm not doing so good. I was wondering if I could come and stay with you for a few days."

He pauses for a few beats. "Does your mother know where you are?"

"No, but I'll tell her as soon as I get a hold of her."

Grandpa clears his throat. "And your father?"

I didn't think this through. I can't tell the truth, but any lie I tell could be debunked with a single phone call. I search for a reason I can't stay with him, and then it hits me. "Well, he and Julia are having a baby, and the baby stuff kind of took over the guest bedroom."

I trace patterns on the crocheted blanket that is draped over the couch I'm sitting on while I wait for him to decide. I count to twelve before he answers me.

"Of course you're welcome here," he says. "Do you have anyone who could give you a ride? My eyesight's not quite what it used to be."

I press the phone against my chest and ask Mrs. Doss, "Could you please give me a ride to my grandpa's house?"

"Of course. You'll just have to give me a few minutes to get ready."

"I've got a ride. Thank you so much, Grandpa. I really appreciate it."

"No problem."

After hanging up the phone, I sigh in relief. I won't be able to go home and pack my toothbrush and pajamas, but I can probably get by for the night.

CHAPTER 39

Beyond the Glass

(A. Child, 2019, pp. 101–102)

It is hard for me to imagine what growing up in Gerald's family was like. When you are little, you imagine that everyone's family is just like yours. Allow me a little narrative intrusion here to share a bit of my life so that you may understand the lens that I am seeing through.

My family was not wealthy but full of love.

Look at that word.

Love.

What do you think it means?

Providing the very best for your children in terms of material things?

Supporting your family through thick and thin?

Being always present for your loved ones?

My parents were able to fulfill all of these. My father worked as hard as he could to support us, but he tried to spend quality time at home when he could. Mom was always there, cooking unicorn-shaped pancakes or my favorite mac and cheese, and we'd watch Nick at Nite together, laughing at *Mr. Ed* and cheered by *Lassie*. Even though my dad wasn't there all the time, I thought our family was perfect, and I thought my parents felt that way, too.

But what if my childhood wasn't like that?

What if my father drank like a fish and beat my mother when she dared disobey him?

Would I have turned out differently?

Maybe I wouldn't become a serial killer, but I could have gotten into more trouble, maybe abused substances to escape from my home life. I could have gotten pregnant and dropped out of high school, gotten into a terrible relationship and fought with my husband all the time, neglected my children rather than go to college and graduate with honors. In that scenario, I wouldn't have followed my dream of writing.

I would have been stuck in a hole.

Just as Gerald felt he was.

That's what gets me when it comes to the nature-versus-nurture argument.

We're all so close to desolation.

Somehow the lucky ones dodge it, while others embrace the darkness.

CHAPTER 40

Gabby

Iowa City, 2024

WHEN WE PULL up to my grandfather's house, I think about my mom's idyllic childhood, how she described her life before her mother died. What must it have been like to live here in the little old ranch with the peeling blue paint and the fence my grandmother painted in rainbow colors. Mom says he's never been able to find someone he loved as much as his late wife. It's romantic, I think, but he must be so lonely. I vow to visit him more often when all of this is said and done.

Mrs. Doss pulls up into the driveway and we both sit there looking at the house before I get out of the car.

"My grandmother was a painter," I explain.

Mrs. Doss nods.

"Do you want me to come with you?"

I shake my head. "Nah, I'll be fine."

She waits for me to ring the doorbell and my grandfather to come to the door before she leaves. He doesn't come out right away, but when he does, an overwhelming smoky smell emanates from within the house. He's wearing an apron that says "Kiss the Cook" on it.

"Gabby, it's so good to see you!" He hugs me and pats me on the back with one hand in an oven mitt. "I tried to make you some cookies, but they burned a little."

He looks me over, and I feel like he's going to tell me how much I've grown since I last saw him, but he refrains.

"Where are your things?" my grandfather asks when Mrs. Doss is gone.

How much should I tell him?

Surely he knows about my mother's book and all the research she did, putting her in danger from all the nutjobs who worship Gerald Shapiro. Do I tell him that there's a new guy out there, kidnapping girls and strangling them? Do I tell him about Bridget? I decide to wait on the nitty gritty details for when I've settled in.

He leads me to my mother's old bedroom, and I feel like I've crawled inside another world. It's pink and scattered with all manner of things—boxes of CDs and magazines, makeup in Caboodles organizers, a closet full of ripped jeans and band t-shirts. It was the nineties, and she was cool. She was strong. She was an aspiring journalist. If only she had known where this path would take her.

I look through the little shelf of books by her bed, wondering if I'll find a stray copy of *Beyond the Glass*, but it's nowhere to be seen. There are a lot of horror novels by authors like Stephen King, along with biographies of musical artists like Kurt Cobain. I'd forgotten that she covered the music beat for her college newspaper. Looking at a person's bookshelf is like crawling into their brain, understanding them a little bit better by the stories they lost themselves in. From my mother's collection, you could see that she is dreamy and creative with just a touch of darkness in her.

My clothes are wet from the snow, so I strip and grab a flannel shirt and jeans from the closet. As I am rummaging through the closet, I see a delicately carved wooden box. I carry it over to the bed and sit cross-legged, debating whether or not to open it.

Secrets have not served us well, I decide.

I open the box and gasp.

My grandfather comes to my door with towels and a washcloth, and he finds me with pictures spread out all over the bed. One woman is in all of them, a woman that I recognize.

It is my grandmother.

"Oh, no! I didn't think, didn't remember those were in there."

I hold up a picture of a pretty brunette in a yellow sundress. She's sitting on the edge of a dock, a 1000-watt smile turned up at the camera.

This exact picture is in my mother's book.

My grandmother.

"Why do you keep these hidden away?" I ask.

As if realizing he is not getting out of this conversation, he sighs and comes into the room, setting the linens down and sitting down next to them. He takes the photograph out of my hands and stares at it for a long moment.

"Lord, she was beautiful."

I riffle through the rest of the pictures and notice two others of my grandmother that showed up in my mother's book.

"Wait," I say. "This is what the two of you were fighting about, isn't it?"

"You're a smart girl," my grandfather says. "I was against it from the beginning. It seemed exploitative to me. We didn't need to make money off our tragedy. If it were up to me, she would have picked something nice to write about, not something that would pull our family into the spotlight to be gawked at."

I have to admit, he has a point about exposing my grandmother to the public as one of Gerald Shapiro's victims. Now, people don't really know anything about her other than she was murdered by the original Catfish Killer. I can see his point.

I gaze down at the pictures and spot something I didn't notice before. In each one, she is wearing a tiny, delicate cross necklace, just like mine.

No, it *is* mine.

I finger the necklace around my neck. "This belonged to her?"

My grandfather straightens his bifocals and looks more closely. "Where did you get it?"

"My mother gave it to me for confirmation."

"Well, I'll be. That's the one . . ." His face goes pale. "We got it back from the police after that . . . that monster was arrested. He'd been keeping it as a souvenir." Suddenly, he seems to come back to himself and realize what he said. "I'm sorry, I shouldn't have told you that."

The necklace seems heavier, searing as though it's burning my neck. But I don't want to take it off. It makes me feel closer to my grandmother. But it makes everything seem so much more real.

"Mom's on her way to see Gerald Shapiro today."

My grandfather's eyes widen. "Is someone there with her?"

I nod. "Law enforcement."

"Why would she want to get involved with this stuff again? It tore her apart the first time. It tore all of us apart."

I marvel at the fact my mother could keep such vital information from her father. But then I think about my own father, and how my trust in him eroded away after he took up with Julia. Since then, I don't tell him much of anything important about my life. Maybe my mother feels the same way about her father and she stopped sharing important things with him after their fight. It's up to me to fill him in.

"A girl from my school is missing," I explain.

"That girl from the news? Such a tragedy. Have they found her yet?"

I shake my head. "That's what Mom is trying to do. Her and Isaac."

He nods solemnly.

"Let's get you set up for bed," he says, patting my knee and then standing. "Here are your towels and things. And I see that you've raided your mother's old closet."

"Why do you keep it like this?" I ask, curiosity crowding out my politeness. "I mean, it's been decades. Why don't you pack it all up and make it into an office or something?"

He is quiet for a moment. "This way, she is still here in some small way. You wouldn't understand."

I think of my father's apartment and the guest bedroom that's being converted into a nursery, basically erasing my existence. "No, I think I do. And I think that's lovely."

After I eat some soup, I crawl into bed and pull up the sheets.

I think about how we can be a different person to everyone we meet in life. My mother was a daughter, a wife, and obviously a mom. But she was someone else to everyone who has ever read her book. Someone else to Gerald Shapiro.

As I drift to sleep, I wonder which version of her will come back to me.

CHAPTER

41

Beyond the Glass

(A. Child, 2019, pp. 106–107)

One of Gerald Shapiro's favorite hobbies was tormenting the people in the families he destroyed. He wrote them letters, describing their loved one's death, what they said, how they begged. He sent them pictures.

Our family was no different. At first he just sent the letters to my father. He included the copies of his online chats with my mother to rub salt in the wound. My father never talked about them, only handed them over to the police to aid in their search.

But one day, when I was a teenager, I got to the mailbox before my father, who was working late. I saw the envelope that was missing a return address and, heart pounding, took it into my room to contemplate. The envelope was a normal business size, with our address printed in careful letters, blood red. It scared me that he had our address, that he could watch us from afar, that he kept tabs on us. The thought chilled me to the bone.

I sat on my bed, staring at the envelope.

Something inside me said don't open it.

But there was something else inside me, the nagging need to *know*.

That was the impulse that drove me to open the letter.

Only it wasn't just a letter.

There were photos.

I looked at the first one, of my mother lying on her back on a bed of leaves, her eyes wide and unseeing. When I realized what it was, I threw the letter and the rest of the pictures off my bed and ran to the bathroom, retching. I stayed there for a long time, watching the water fill the sink. I let it fill to the very top and then splashed it on my face, wanting to feel the cool water, wanting to feel anything other than how the picture made me feel.

When my father got home, he found the pictures on the kitchen table, where I left them. He came into my room with a pained expression.

"You saw," he said.

It wasn't a question.

He sat down on the bed next to me and pulled me over to him, wrapping his arms around me. It didn't comfort me. It wasn't enough. I would have done anything to go back and not open the envelope. I wanted to bleach my brain, to unsee what I saw.

Unfortunately, there was no way to do that, and there was no way to stop Gerald from harassing us with those letters for the remaining years that I lived with my father. When I went to college, I majored in journalism and focused on writing about true crime and serial killers, specifically my mother's killer. I needed to learn more about how they operated.

I needed to learn *why* they did what they did.

CHAPTER

42

Amelia

Newton Correctional Facility, 2024

It's been a long time since I set foot in a prison. I've spent more time than I care to admit behind these locked doors, interviewing Gerald Shapiro. It all feels eerily familiar as I take off my earrings, shoes, and belt for the metal detector and let the guard go through my purse to make sure I don't have a shiv or other contraband. I forget to take my phone out of my purse, but the guard seizes it and puts it in a bin for me to retrieve before we leave the jail.

Isaac is waiting for me beyond the metal detector. I step back into my shoes and grab my purse. "He knows we're coming?" I ask.

Isaac nods. "I called ahead. He should be waiting for us."

Sure enough, he is.

As we walk through the door, his eyes lock on mine. I feel the breath knocked out of me as I face my mother's killer once again.

He has aged significantly since I saw him ten years ago. Prison has not treated him well. The last time I talked to him, he still had a full head of blonde hair. Now it's gone gray and is receding. He has developed deep lines in his face, most noticeably around his mouth, like he's been smoking a pack a day. His once-piercing blue eyes have faded, although I'm sure he's still sharp as a tack.

"Remember what we said," Isaac says, referring to our plan of letting him do the talking and me doing the listening. I have a tape recorder, ready to go. It's strange that we'll be discussing a kidnapping in progress rather than stories from the past to go into a book. I don't want to give him the satisfaction of that idea, that someone is following in his footsteps.

The guard standing behind us hits a button, and a horn blasts, indicating the door is being opened. Inside the room, Gerald sits on one side of the steel table, his chained hands laced together. I know it's one of the rules, to keep us safe as we do our work. I try not to think about what those hands could do to me if he were let loose.

Isaac pulls out a chair for me, and I sit down.

"Ooh, so gentlemanly," Gerald says snidely.

Isaac takes his seat and slides a large manila folder onto the table in front of him. Inside are pictures of Bridget, the place where she was abducted, pictures of the copy of *Beyond the Glass* that she'd been reading.

"We're going to keep this short and sweet," Isaac says. "In and out."

"That's what she said," Gerald says, leering at me.

Isaac does not let Gerald get to him.

"We are here because of a recent abduction. Do you recognize this girl?" Isaac slides it across the table for Gerald to examine.

Gerald stares at the photograph of Bridget blankly.

"I don't know who this is."

"The hell you don't," Isaac says. "It's your MO, kidnapping defenseless girls. And this one seemed to be obsessed with you. Look at that book she was reading."

"I'm not saying you're wrong," Gerald replies. "But I really don't know what this is."

There's something in Gerald's eyes that strikes me as genuine, but I remind myself he's a pro at this. During his trial, he maintained a constant refusal that he did any of the crimes. The prosecutor had a hard time getting him to talk. It was like pulling teeth.

Gerald smirks. "Can I help it if I have a lot of fans?"

"This is not just a fan," Isaac says. "This is a girl who is going to be dead very soon, if you don't help us find the copycat."

Gerald shrugs. "Not my circus, not my monkeys."

This interrogation is not going the way I hoped it would. Gerald is a total narcissist. If he had anything to do with Bridget's kidnapping, he would say that he's behind it, if only for the press coverage.

"Do you know the man who's doing this?" Isaac asks.

"I just told you, I have nothing to do with it," Gerald insists. He turns to me. "Amelia, how have you been? I think about you a lot in here. You and your family."

His tone is menacing.

I'm not supposed to talk, but he is infuriating me and I think I might be able to get him to crack. After all, the only reason people know his name is because of me and the book I wrote.

"Don't you talk about my family," I say, slamming my hand down on the table. The sound sends an echo throughout the room. Gerald seems surprised at the intensity of the noise I created. "Tell us what happened to this girl."

"I'm telling you the truth, buttercup. If I did it, I'd take credit for it. You know that about me."

He's got a point. If there was any chance in hell that Gerald is the one behind this, he'd be crowing from the rooftops about how he could wreak havoc, even from behind bars.

"If you're not behind it," I say, "then who is?"

"A lot of people could have done it," he says, examining his nails. "Practically anyone. As you said, I've got a lot of fans. I hang their letters up in my cell. It brings me joy, to know that others have been inspired by my work."

The word "inspired" pisses me off.

"Inspired? Inspired by what? Kidnapping women, raping them, strangling them to death? If what you say is true and people are enjoying that shit, I am very worried about this world." My words are poison, I hurl them at him.

Gerald throws me an amused look. "Aren't you being a little hypocritical, hon?"

"What do you mean?"

"I mean that you're the one who made me into a star. If people just read about me in the newspapers, I would be a train wreck, an anecdote one discusses at the water cooler at work. But you made me into something more than that, all your psychological mumbo jumbo. People are fascinated by me. They want to know what makes me tick. People are obsessed with me, starting fan clubs in my honor. All because of you."

The words sting. He has a point. By shedding light on Gerald Shapiro, I made him into a celebrity.

"You know, hon," he says. "You should be home with your family. Let the cops figure this one out. You'll just make yourself sick with it."

Another reference to my family. Is he referring to what he did to my mom so long ago? Is he suggesting that I might be in danger? Or Gabby? No, I won't let him distract me from finding out who the hell is behind Bridget's kidnapping.

"Are you sure you don't know anyone who could be responsible for this?" Isaac jumps back in to save me from Gerald's psychological torture. "What about your son?"

Gerald doesn't enjoy having the game turned back on him. He scowls at Isaac. "You leave him alone," Gerald says. "He's made his own life for himself, and he likes to keep it private. He has nothing to do with this."

"We know where he is. Do you have anything you'd like us to pass along?"

But Gerald's mouth is sealed closed, his eyes narrowed. It makes me think of what my mother must have seen during her last moments.

I stand up, spit at him, and turn to leave the room.

CHAPTER 43

Beyond the Glass

(A. Child, 2019, pp. 107–109)

After Gerald Shapiro was arrested, he came clean with everything.

Every crime, every victim.

He wanted it all documented, and I suppose in a way he used me as much as I used him to clarify what happened to my mother. He wanted credit for what he'd done, now that he was behind bars for good.

I think he enjoyed describing the details of his killings to me. He took sadistic pleasure in his retellings, lingering on tidbits like last words and how long it took to strangle each girl. How he arranged them, what he was going for artistically. He laid it all out there for me.

He also liked to talk about other serial killers and how he compared to them. He'd list names and number of kills like he was discussing the local sports team's wins and losses. He was very careful to make sure I understood that he was the very best at what he did. Other killers were stupid, didn't know what they were doing. He explained how they could have avoided being caught, never acknowledging that he was manipulated into showing himself.

Gerald had an ego, and he was competitive.

He'd never let anyone outshine him.

CHAPTER

44

The Kidnapper

Homestead, 2024

To pass the time, I go to the Free Gerry website discussion forum to see if anybody's posted anything new about Gerald Shapiro. Lots of people who knew him on the outside come here to post memories and tidbits about his life growing up. One time, his former neighbor claimed he was always looking in her window at night. Another time, a man said Gerald had saved his life by hoisting him back onto a bridge when he tried to jump. I don't know which stories are true, but it's interesting to learn about all the different sides to him.

There's a guard who works at the prison who updates us on what he's been reading or talking about lately. Sometimes he relays our messages to Gerald, lets him know that we're thinking about him and that all is not lost. Maybe that last appeal fell through, but there will be others. Stuff like that.

There's a new thread called "Iowa Girl Missing." My heart pounding, I click on it. The page opens up with a comment including a picture of the girl who is currently in my basement. Looks like it was ripped off from her Instagram. Turns out the guard did post it, and he's got a message to go with it.

GERRY WANTS TO KNOW WHO DID THIS.

A thrill rushes through me as I see the message on the discussion forum.

He knows.

Gerald Shapiro knows what I have done.

And I can't keep from wanting him to know who I am.

Of course, I can't just come out and announce my identity, no matter how much I'd bask in the glory of the knowledge that my idol knows I exist. But maybe I could just post a little something to hint that I know where the girl is. From a different account? Using a VPN? The website claims not to collect that sort of information, anyway.

I log out of my current account, username GOATCK (Greatest of All-Time Catfish Killer), and create an email address for a new account. Chewing my thumbnail, I try to think of an inconspicuous username. Maybe a nod to one of Gerald Shapiro's kills back in the day. Perhaps the mother of the famous Amelia Child. I type in ANOTHERCHILD and make up a bunch of shit for the rest of my profile.

Then I add my comment to the thread.

"I did."

My heart is pounding, and I hit "Post" before slamming my computer shut and taking a moment to catch my breath. Adrenaline is coursing through my veins, and I have to get up and walk around the room to settle myself down. Then a banging noise interrupts my thoughts, and I turn in irritation, realizing that my hostage is demanding attention again. I suppose she wants to be fed or taken to the potty like a toddler. I almost regret keeping her around, but the money will be nice when it comes through. And then I can dispose of her.

I find a can of expired tuna in the recesses of one of the cabinets, and I'm glad to see that Renee remembered to stock the kitchen with a can opener. I take a halfway clean glass and fill it with water, turning to the basement door once more. Before I go down, I don my mask.

Downstairs, the girl stops banging on the pipe when she sees me with food. She makes a face when she sees the can of tuna, but that's just too bad. Beggars can't be choosers. I put it on the ground and push it over to her with my foot, wait until she eats it instead of kicking it aside, as she did with my last offering. She reluctantly scoops out a little tuna fish and eats it off her finger before devouring it in a couple bites, having determined it is safe.

"Have they sent the money?" she asks through a mouthful.

"It's going to take them some time," I reply.

She lets out a shuddering sigh. "But they're going to be able to get it?"

"Apparently."

I turn to leave when she speaks again. "What are you going to do with me?" There's real curiosity in her voice. I study her. She shrinks back, and it sends a little jolt of pleasure through me, her fear. It's delicious. I try not to think about what to do with her once her parents pay. No dessert before supper.

"I haven't decided yet."

"You know, I read about people like you," she says cautiously.

"What do you mean, people like me?"

"I mean, I read a lot of true crime. I know you're not going to just give me back to my parents. That's not how it works."

"You think you know so much?" I ask with disdain. "You know nothing about me."

"I was reading a book from the library," she says. "It was about a man who kidnapped girls, just like you. He kept them in their basement, just like you. The only difference is that he took pictures of them." She stops talking abruptly, like she doesn't want to give me any ideas.

My mouth goes dry. She couldn't be talking about—

"What book?" I demand.

"*Beyond the Glass*. It was about this guy who met girls online and catfished them to get them to meet up. And then he took them to his so-called photography studio and . . . and . . ."

"Strangled them," I finish for her.

It's impossible that the girl could have been reading that book, my bible. A coincidence, for sure. Or maybe it's not. One of her classmate's mothers wrote the book. That's enough to make anyone curious. The idea makes me feel exposed somehow, like she's gotten into my brain, like she knows my next move. I don't like it. I try to think of something to get back in control of the situation, maybe give her a taste of what she's thinking is going to happen.

"Okay," I say, fishing my phone out of my pocket. I raise it to eye level and take a picture of her, sitting there, pathetic with her little can of tuna.

"What are you doing?" she asks.

"For your parents," I reply, taking another. "Gotta show them you're alive. Otherwise they won't pay me."

"Stop it," she pleads. "I don't want them to see me like this."

"If you resist, I have several ideas of how I could persuade you," I suggest.

The implied threat hangs in the air.

"Okay," she says meekly.

Looking through the camera lens, I say, "Scrunch up a little more. Like you're scared."

"I am scared," she replies.

I take a step forward, draw my arm up as though I'm going to hit her again.

She flinches.

"Better," I say, and I crouch down to take a few more shots. For one I get up close, focusing on her face. "You know what would make this more convincing? A little blood. That would signal how serious I am about this whole thing."

The thought is enough to bring terror to her face, and I take another series of photos.

"Good," I say finally, straightening and scrolling through the photos I just took.

They'll do.

I look around and see that she has picked up a few of the spy thrillers that fell on the floor when she was kicking the pipe. "I see you've found some reading material. How are you liking them? Not as intense as your true crime books, I suppose."

She just stares at me.

"I've got a copy of that book you were talking about. It inspires me. Because it's an exploration of the dark side of humanity. So often people don't realize how good they have it. *Beyond the Glass* presents a museum of horrors that shows the extent of human depravity, so often hidden in day-to-day life."

"It's terrifying," she says.

I nod in agreement. "That's what makes it so great. Maybe someday your story will be told, just like the ones in that book."

CHAPTER

45

Beyond the Glass

(A. Child, 2020, pp. 112–116)

Imagine hearing the story of your mother's death from the mouth of her very killer. It might make you nauseous, it might speed up your heart. You might want to sharpen an axe to take off his head. But then you start to realize this is the only way you're going to get any answers. And so you screw up your courage and go see them. And this is what they tell you.

Gerald was prepared. He'd scouted out the spot beforehand. Made sure the cemetery would be vacated. It was surrounded by woods, the perfect place for him to execute his plan.

I wonder what she was thinking on the ride there. Maybe she was wishing she'd taken the time to let her husband know she was going to be late for dinner. It's hard to imagine that she didn't have any intuition that something bad was going to happen.

Gerald described the graveyard as pretty, with tombstones arranged in straight lines like rows of white marble teeth, secluded from the rest of the world. Off to one side of the graveyard was the tree line of a small forest. Rather than looking dark and dreary, though, the woods seemed festive, showcasing flaming autumnal leaves. A number of them had fallen to the ground. The red and orange leaves that crunched beneath their feet made him feel as though they were walking through fire.

Elaine followed him through the cemetery, and he said that it was apparent that she was getting scared. He got off on that part, being in control of another human's feelings. But she didn't turn back. It was as if she was determined to prove to herself that Gerald was a nice guy, just a little strange from lack of human contact.

Exactly when did she feel something was wrong? That she'd made a mistake?

"Gerald?" she said, her voice shaking.

He didn't stop, just turned his head to the side to tell her to come on. She kept walking. Soon they were at the very edge of the woods, and he stopped and turned around to face her.

"Where is it?" Elaine asked, looking around for a tombstone with his wife's name, but there was nothing. He could see the realization all over her face. Was she scolding herself for being so gullible? Was she afraid about what was about to happen?

She took a step back when he didn't answer.

He reached out and grabbed a fistful of her hair.

"Don't," she begged. "Please don't hurt me. I have a husband and a daughter. They'll realize I'm gone. They'll call the police. In fact, I'm sure they already have."

Gerald knew it was bullshit.

Elaine began to scream. "Please, someone! Help!"

But there was no one else in the cemetery, and they were too far away for anyone to hear on the street. Holding his hand over her mouth, he wrapped his free arm around her chest, spinning her around and holding her close to his chest. He let go of her hair with a hand still clamped over her mouth. He dragged her into the trees, far enough back that no one would see.

It was cold outside, and she was shivering as he took down her pants. She turned away, but Gerald grabbed her face and turned it toward him. He wanted to see her break.

The clouds parted, and the sun shone down on them.

When he was finished, he saw the gleam of hope in her eyes. Maybe he was done. Perhaps she could still get out of this alive.

He wanted to extinguish any inkling that she was anything but a toy for him to play with and discard.

He let her pull her jeans back up and button them. He was behind her, and he saw her prepare to run away. Angry, he picked up a rock and slammed it into the back of her head. She was down for the count, and he climbed onto her again, wrapping his hands around her throat.

"Got any last words?" he asked, letting up a little, just enough for her to speak.

She hesitated, and then she said, "Tell my daughter I love her."

Curiously, he searched her eyes. "You want me to talk to your daughter?"

Surely, that wasn't what she wanted.

"Don't talk to her, but somehow, let her know that I love her."

He squeezed then, as tightly as he could, and watched the light go out of her eyes.

But he remembered the promise.

CHAPTER 46

Amelia

Iowa City, 2000

M<small>Y MOTHER'S FUNERAL</small> was surreal. There were plainclothes police officers scattered among the crowd, which freaked me out at first, until my father explained that they were looking for the killer, that often killers will show up at their victims' funerals. They want to see what havoc they caused. It's all about ego for them. They are cocky, careless. They will try to hide in plain sight.

It made me paranoid, looking around the room and wondering whether any of these men was my mother's murderer. The problem was that everyone looked so normal. There was no villain in a cape, hiding behind a curtain somewhere. It made me feel guilty because most of the crowd was there because they were genuinely upset that my mother was killed in such a brutal way.

We were Catholic, and though we didn't go to the church often, I was comforted by it all. Everything shiny and gold. Statues of saints. A giant crucified Christ on the altar in front. Little bowls of water to dip my fingers in to cleanse my soul before I could defile it with my sins. All of these things to keep the monsters away.

But I was angry. What good did believing in God do for my mother, when she was so horrifically ripped from this earth, from me and my dad? I was too mad to cry. I sat shredding tissues in my sweating hands, wishing I had been the one to die instead of my mother.

Suddenly, I felt someone watching me. I turned my head slightly and saw a tall guy with blonde hair staring at me. There was something wrong about him. He didn't look sad. He looked . . . curious. I thought about pointing him out to my dad, but he was in his own world of sorrow, and I didn't want to add to his woe.

Someone started to play the piano, and the priest walked up the aisle holding a bible in front of him. Everyone hushed and watched him take the steps up to the altar, rest the Bible on the pulpit, and adjust the microphone. Everyone but that man. He watched me.

"We are gathered here today for a heartbreaking reason. One of us has been stolen from this life too soon."

A woman behind me sobbed.

"Elaine Child was an incredible woman. Wife, mother, daughter. So many people loved her, as we can see here today," gesturing to the mass of people spilling out of pews. The place had filled up so much since I came in that there were people leaning against the wall, listening intently to the priest.

"Not only was this an untimely death, but a senseless one. It's hard to understand how someone could steal the life of such a promising, loving soul."

Someone passed a note down the aisle. My name was on it. I unfolded the paper, and it said, in jagged, almost childlike, handwriting: "She loved you."

I looked back to see if the man was still there, but he was gone.

CHAPTER 47

Gabby

Iowa City, 2024

I'VE BEEN COOPED up in my mother's old bedroom, too scared to leave my grandfather's house after seeing that note. He made me a breakfast of muffins and fresh fruit and brought it to me on a tray, somehow sensing that I just wanted to stay in my mother's room, curved into a ball. I don't want to tell him about the warning; he's been through enough without me bothering him with what is probably just a practical joke.

But I need my mother. Even if she didn't tell me about her mother, I still need her to make everything okay. When my grandfather brings me lunch, I ask him if she's called yet.

"No, I'm sorry," he says, nudging the tray onto the nightstand. "I did talk with your father. He wants to know what's going on. I told him I'd have you call him."

When he leaves, I turn on the antique television. I flip it to the news channel to see if there have been any new developments. There's one interview with Bridget's parents. I turn up the volume and flop down on my stomach to watch. The mother looks a lot like Bridget, with dark hair and blue eyes, although hers are lined with red. It doesn't look like she's gotten much sleep, which is understandable.

Her husband has a dull brown head of hair, a mustache, and a cleft chin. He pleads for the kidnapper to spare their baby girl. Something about him gives me an eerie chill that goes up and down my back. I can feel goosebumps pop up on my arms. He doesn't even look sad. His face is very matter of fact. But he can't be responsible for this. Not when there was a truck identified that most definitely belonged to someone else. But could he know something and he's not letting on?

The more I think about it, the more creeped out I get.

I dig out my computer and navigate to Instagram, where I find Bridget's account, which she has set to public. There are a lot of memes and pictures of photographs from various concerts she's been to. I click on her followers and scroll through the list, not sure what I'm looking for. Are the newest followers at the top or the bottom? Or are they in no order at all?

I click back on Bridget's account and look at it even more closely. There is a selfie shot she took from above with her laptop in the background behind her. It's some website, but I can't tell what it is. I click on the image and zoom in to try and make it out.

When I enlarge it, though, I see it's a website entitled, "Free Gerry." There are a couple of pictures of Gerald Shapiro in the banner and a list of over 6,000 followers supporting his cause. I knew there were creepers out there, writing fan letters to Gerald, but I never imagined he'd have this many. And why was Bridget checking it out?

When I type the website into Google, it brings up a page with a banner in red and white reading "Free Gerry." It has a picture of Gerald Shapiro from a long time ago. My stomach drops. Is this the shit she was into? Maybe he really does have something to do with her disappearance. In the photos that line the left side of the web page, there are multiple pictures of various people holding signs that say "Free Gerry" on them. There's even a link to order a t-shirt with the slogan on it.

It makes me sick.

In order to access the forums within the site, I have to create an account. There's no way I'm using my school email to get into this psycho-fest, so I whip one up on Gmail named "FuckGerry" and then click on the forums. The threads vary from specific crimes he was accused of to a recent one discussing a new abduction. Bridget's abduction. My stomach lurches.

I click on it and read comment after comment of people speculating that it was committed by Gerald's copycat, who seems to be responsible for a dozen killings around the Midwest in the past couple years. Halfway down the page, there's a post that simply reads, "Gerry wants to know who did this." I can't believe it. Gerald has a connection with the outside world, someone who is commenting on his fan website. And he wants to know what's going on. As in *he doesn't know what's going on.*

A few comments below that, someone called "Another-Child" says, "I did."

I pause and stare at the words, my heart beating fast, my stomach feeling sick. What kind of a person would post this? It surely can't be real. It has to be some sort of troll, messing with the people on the forum.

But then I start to second-guess myself. If the message from the prison guard is real, maybe this one is, too. I remember the chapter from my mom's book. The one all about Gerald Shapiro's ego. I don't think he'd like someone posing as him, killing women and posing them like he did in his reign of terror. Maybe this is a point of pride, someone taking credit for his work in the only way he knows how. If so, this could be how we find Bridget.

CHAPTER 48

Amelia

Omaha, 2024

I'M STARVING BY the time we reach Omaha to see Simon. We decide to stop at a gas station restaurant to grab some burgers, and we sit in a booth while we wait for our order to come up. I drop my head into my hands, rubbing my temples. I've got a headache coming on.

Isaac starts to rub my back. "I know that wasn't easy, facing Gerald again."

"That's the understatement of the year."

He leans in to give me a gentle kiss. "I'm proud of you. That's what I admire about you; you're the strongest person I've ever known. Even in the face of such evil."

I grimace. "I don't feel that way."

"Come here," he says, pulling me close. His arms around me feel so solid, like something to cling to in a storm, but they still don't take away the image of Gerald's sneering face. I feel something vibrate in Isaac's jacket pocket.

"Damn it," he says, pulling it from his pocket and checking the number. "I've gotta take this."

I sigh and move away, listening to his side of the conversation, praying it's good news.

"Uh-huh . . . Okay . . . I understand . . ."

When he hangs up the phone, his face is grim. "The kidnapper has contacted Bridget's parents. He's asking for a ransom."

I pause, running my fingers through my hair.

"Well, at least we know she's alive, right?"

"I wouldn't say that for sure, but he did send some pictures in which she appeared to be alive. Very scared, but alive."

"So what happens next?" I ask.

Isaac sits up straight, smoothing his uniform. "We told her parents to ask him for some time, so we can pinpoint where he is. They did an interview on the news, to keep people looking."

"Are you going to release the information about the ransom?"

"We're holding it close to the vest for right now."

We are both quiet for a moment, lost in our own thoughts. I gather my strength to stand up. "Well, we'd better go see about Simon. There's no time to waste."

He nods, and we head for the door without getting our food.

CHAPTER

49

Gabby

Iowa City, 2024

Despite my fight with Easton, he's the only one I want to share my discovery on the message board with. I use my grandpa's landline to call him, and he grudgingly agrees to come over. It's strange seeing Easton in my mom's old bedroom.

Normally, we'd have our hands all over each other, but it's not exactly the time or the place. Nevertheless, my grandfather has insisted I leave the door wide open, and he shuffles in every once in a while to offer us tea or cookies.

Easton sits on the bed next to me, but he's a full six inches away from me as I describe what I've discovered. I open my laptop and show him the Free Gerry website, and his eyes widen when he sees the post about Gerald wanting to know who took Bridget. When I show him the post where another user claims to have done it, he looks dubious.

"I don't know, Gabs. It seems a little far-fetched. It's probably just some troll trying to take credit to get a thrill out of the whole thing."

"There's only one way to find out," I say, and I click on the button to create a new account. The only way to catch a catfish is to catfish them back. And the FuckGerry persona is not going to cut it.

He presses his lips together and shakes his head. "I don't think it's a great idea. If you're right, we could stir him up, make him do something bad to Bridget if he hasn't already."

"I disagree," I say. "The worst thing we can do is nothing. It's a terrible scenario already. Gerald's copycat has taken Bridget, and he could off her at any time. We need to act fast."

At my earnest voice, Easton reaches out and brushes a hair out of my eyes. "Okay, I get it. But what kind of a person would the copycat want to talk to?"

I consider the question. Maybe someone meek and unthreatening, like Bridget? Possible prey, another pretty girl that he could go after when he's finished with Bridget? I could find an attractive picture online and upload it to get him excited. If we are careful, we could get him to expose himself in some way, give us enough evidence to show to Isaac. But why would he open up like that to a random girl? Also, whatever account I create is going to show that it was made today, just like his.

Why did he comment on this post anyway? The only thing I can figure is that he was so enticed by the idea that the mighty Gerald Shapiro was asking about where the girl was.

And then, a flash of inspiration.

If he thinks Gerald is watching him, why not create a persona that could be Gerald in disguise, reaching out to find out what the kidnapper is up to?

I run the idea by Easton, and he looks doubtful, but he likes it better than the idea of pretending to be a woman coming on to the monster.

Pondering what I should call my new persona, I think back to my mother's book. What's a fact about Gerald that no one would know unless they were intimately familiar with his history? The copycat referenced our family. Should I do the same? Play on the Child theme? Or should I take the family idea and flip it on its head, refer to Gerald's family in some way?

What were his parents' names, anyway? I close my eyes and try to remember that early chapter in the book that explored his childhood. Tim? Tim and Sheila? That doesn't seem right. No, it was Tom. Tom. Tomboy. Tom's boy.

Tom's boy.

That's it. Gerald is Tom's first son, and the copycat would know it, like everything else he knows about the original serial killer. I create the account and fill in the name blank with TomsBoy1. The rest of the information I fill out with gibberish. I don't upload a picture. It doesn't really matter, anyway. The copycat will know this is a throwaway account, just like AnotherChild. Within seconds, I click enter and the account is complete.

"Are you ready?" I ask Easton.

"What are you going to write?" he replies, chewing his nail.

He's right to be nervous. We have to be careful. If I'm correct, it's a straight method of communication that I have with Bridget's kidnapper. I probably should let my mom and Isaac know what I'm doing, but it's such a reach that I want to make sure I'm right before I tell them.

Finally, in true catfish spirit, I slide into his inbox with a provocative message.

"You want to talk to me, huh?"

That should get his attention.

With a trembling finger, I hit send.

Easton and I stare at the page for a while, hoping for a little red notification to pop up, but nothing happens, and it very quickly becomes incredibly boring. I minimize the web page and pull up the local news channel, which we watch, waiting for updates.

It has "breaking news" streaming along the bottom of the screen, and the video is of the local chief of police doing a press conference. Bridget's parents have come forward with pictures sent from an anonymous source. She's in a fetal position, looking miserable. They are hoping someone will recognize some detail about her surroundings and would be able to help find her. Everyone in the media is going mad. If they weren't all over the case already, they sure are in the game now.

"Jesus Christ," Easton says after seeing a picture of Bridget with an angry bruise over one cheekbone. "If we find him, I'm going to tear him limb from limb." His hands are clenched.

I suddenly realize this is Easton's ex-girlfriend we're talking about. I haven't even taken his feelings into account about what's happening.

"Easton, are you okay?"

He takes a ragged breath. "Not really, no. It's not like I have any romantic feelings for her anymore, but I still care about her. This is so fucked up."

I pull him into a hug. "I know," I whisper into his ear. "We'll find her," I promise. He relaxes into my embrace, and we sit there for a long time.

Something about this kidnapper seems different from the accounts about Gerald Shapiro that my mother outlined in her book. While my mom's book described Gerald as organized, this kidnapper seems sloppy. He took Bridget in a parking lot, where anyone could have seen what was happening if they came out of the coffee shop. Unlike Shapiro, the kidnapper seems to have an ulterior motive beyond just hurting and killing someone. If I had been suspicious of my father before, the feeling fades when I see the pictures of her. No way could he be capable of such violence. It just doesn't make any sense.

I want to hear his voice, reassure myself that he is at home with Julia, not sending weird pictures to Bridget's family. I go into the living room and pick up my grandfather's phone, dialing the numbers carefully. My father picks up on the second ring.

"Gabby, is that you?" He sounds panicked.

I ignore his question and ask my own. "Do you have anything you want to tell me?"

It reminds me of when I was young and spilled Kool-Aid all over his first edition of *The Great Gatsby*. I'd been running around the room and bumped into the coffee table, which the book was laying on. I tried to clean it up with paper towels, but it only made the mess worse. I stuck the book under one of the couch cushions, and my dad was looking for it for weeks. In the end, he asked me that question. *Do you have anything you want to tell me?* It's a great way of digging up deceit because it's vague enough that it will prompt someone to tell you anything they may have been hiding from you.

My father goes quiet. I can hear his breathing on the other line, a bit quicker and harder than usual. He's feeling guilty about something. He *knows* something. But if he wouldn't tell it to my mother, there's no way in hell he'd tell me.

I pull at a loose string on my jeans, not knowing what else to say. Either he tells me or he doesn't. It's out of my hands now. But I'm not sure I can trust him anymore—well, even less than I did before, given that he was cheating on my mom for months before it came out.

"You're still at Grandpa's, right?" My father hesitates. "Because it's actually good you're there. Julia's had some cramping, and we're going to go to the hospital. I'm sure she'll be fine. I just . . . I don't know how long we'll be there, so just stay put, okay?"

"Okay," I reply.

I hold the phone against my chest and breathe out, then put it back in the cradle.

Easton comes up from behind me and wraps his arms around me. "What did he say?"

"Nothing." I shake my head. "He didn't say anything."

I cover my eyes and start to cry. Nothing makes sense to me. Could it really be my father on that website, trying to get Gerald Shapiro's attention?

I lie back on my bed, and Easton curls around me, smoothing my hair back from my face as tears stream down my cheeks. I close my eyes and try to imagine what Bridget is going through. Is she hurt? Is she hungry? Is she scared? I can't get the picture out of my head, the one from my mom's book of the woman with a spike through her head. I know that childhood Gerald was the one to draw that picture, but how far is this guy willing to go to impress his predecessor?

Then I picture my mom, imagine what she would say. Giving up is not an option, not when there's a life on the line. There is a courage inside myself that I never even knew I had. It's the strength to keep going, even when things seem bleak.

I guess I got that quality from my mom.

CHAPTER

50

The Kidnapper

Homestead, 2024

I SHUT OFF THE TV and stare into space, but the image of the girl's parents standing on their front porch, talking to reporters, is burned into my mind. I can't believe I actually thought they were going to give me the money. I was so sure they would find a way.

And they shared the photos I sent! Right now, everyone in the Midwest is probably flipping through them, analyzing the background, wondering if they can figure out what the girl's surroundings can tell them about her whereabouts. I know how these things go. I saw a thing on Netflix about a criminal being caught because of the vacuum cleaner in a video he posted. Online sleuths called around until they found the exact shop where it was sold. People will find an outlet or the pipes or something in the picture I took of Bridget, and somehow they'll track me down. I've got to get rid of the girl, clean my truck thoroughly, and wipe my digital footprint. That at least will be easy enough. I'll start by deleting that stupid post I made on the Free Gerry website.

My gaze falls to my laptop, which lays open on the couch. The Internet fills the screen, and I see that there's a little red notification at the top of the Free Gerry website. Someone has sent me a message. My heart races as I click on it, not knowing what to expect.

The message is from someone called TomsBoyl.

TomsBoyl?

Gerald's father was named Tom.

The message reads, "You want to talk to me, huh?"

Could this actually be Gerald, contacting me somehow? I can't imagine he'd have Internet privileges, but I know there's at least one guard on his side, doing his bidding. It's totally possible that he could have seen my message and felt the need to respond. And if so, maybe he can help me out with my situation. If anyone would know how to get out of this, it would be him.

Still, I must be careful.

I think a moment, and then type a response. "How do I know it's you?"

A few dots appear at the bottom of the message, meaning the message sender is there right now, waiting to talk to yours truly. He's been in my shoes. He can help me.

The words pop onto the screen. "Your handle is a reference to Elaine Child's family, isn't it? How much do you know about her murder?"

I swallow.

"I've done my research."

"I believe you. But what you might not know, what they never told the public, is that I took a souvenir the day I murdered Elaine. I'll bet you have a copy of that book, *Beyond the Glass*. Take a look. It's in all of the pictures of Elaine."

My eyes dart to the book lying a few feet away from me on the couch. I pick it up and flip through the pages until I find the chapter about Elaine Child. I look closely and realize she's wearing a cross necklace in each one.

"So what?" I ask.

"So, the necklace got confiscated by police when they arrested me. Now the granddaughter wears it. That's how you can tell who the girl really is. The girl you took isn't wearing that necklace, is she?"

No, of course she isn't wearing that necklace. I took the wrong girl.

But now I believe it really is Gerald Shapiro that I'm talking with.

It's stupid to do what I'm about to do, I know that, but I'm also desperate. I can hear the girl banging in the basement again, and I'm getting a tension headache.

"I'm having some troubles here," I type slowly. "And I'm not sure how to get in control of the situation."

Minutes pass before the dots show up again. Finally, Gerald replies, "I can help you."

The moment of connection, talking to someone who has done this all before and knows what it's like, brings tears to my eyes. I cry like a little girl.

"Please. I'll do anything," I type.

Long moments pass, and I begin to wonder if I've made a mistake. Maybe this is just some random person on the Internet that I've shared my problems with. Or maybe it is Gerald, but he is angry that I'm trying to steal his thunder, replicate the crimes he committed but doing them so poorly that I got myself into this mess.

But then . . .

"Where are you?"

Relief pours through me. I tell him that I'm just outside of Iowa City. Gerald responds that he knows a man who can meet with me in a few hours. He'll be at a cafe in Williamsburg. I gulp in air and try to regulate my breathing. It's going to be okay. I haven't fucked things up too badly, keeping the girl for too long and giving away too much to the media. Gerald knows someone who will help me out of this.

I agree to the meeting. When I close my laptop, I feel so much better. I sit down and think of a way to keep my mind occupied until it's time to head out. I pick up my Xbox controller and lean back in my recliner.

CHAPTER 51

Beyond the Glass

(A. Child, 2019, pp. 143–144)

When Simon was only three, he was punished for lying to his father about taking cookies from the cookie jar. The way Gerald described the situation:

> I'm not sure he was that young. Did he tell you that? Gosh, I haven't thought about this for a long time. Yeah, I guess it must have been about 2008? We had a couple of good years in there. Susan was always cooking something. I looked forward to coming home and smelling my dinner and knowing that there were people actually glad to see me. I'd never really had that before.

Shapiro paused for a moment during this discussion, as if he was choked up. He bent over the table between us and cried into his hands. Only it wasn't crying. It was laughter. Terrible laughter. It was so frightening that I almost had to get up and leave. But eventually he calmed down enough to answer a few more questions.

So back to Simon. Yeah, he was stealing a cookie out of the cookie jar. I'm pretty sure those are the lyrics to some song. Do you know it? I know, I know, I'm avoiding the question. Well, anyway, it was on a Saturday afternoon and Simon wouldn't eat his lunch because the casserole his mother made had green things in it. It just made me real mad, you know. Here's this lady making him a meal and he was rude enough to turn it down?

He said he wanted cookies for lunch instead. I was pissed off, so I grabbed the cookie jar off the fridge and put it on the table in front of him. "Eat," I said. "If you won't eat your lunch, if you really want cookies, then eat."

So he ate one.

"Another one," I told him. "Another."

We kept on going until he barfed all over the kitchen table. He wasn't big enough to clean it up, so I did it, and I was pissed about it for a long while. Every time he made a peep about not liking something we had to eat, I threatened the cookie jar, and he shut up and ate the green things. You've gotta be strict on kids, especially boys, or else they'll run you ragged.

CHAPTER

52

Amelia

Omaha, 2024

Simon's house is a small bungalow painted an off-white color. Or maybe it's supposed to be pure white, but it's just a little bit dirty. There's a black truck in the driveway. When I see it, I nudge Isaac, and he nods. Faded Christmas decorations hang sadly in the yard as if they are there all year round.

As always, Isaac goes first. I'm reassured by his presence. I wonder if maybe, when this is all over, we could be something. Could we be together through the monotony of day-to-day life, when we're not tracking down kidnappers and serial killers? Or are we two desperate souls clinging together in the midst of disaster?

He presses the doorbell, and we wait. Simon comes to the door. He is a small, unassuming man wearing a pair of nylon shorts and a Guardians of the Galaxy shirt. His dark hair is too long and greasy. He has patches of acne on his nose and chin. He looks much younger than he should at twenty, as if something stunted his growth. I have to remind myself that he only lived with Gerald Shapiro for a few years when he was very young, but I imagine that the living situation would be horrific enough to scar anyone who lived with him for any period of time.

"Mr. Shapiro?" Isaac asks.

"I don't want to buy anything," Simon says.

"I don't want to sell anything," Isaac retorts. "But it's in your best interests to give us any insight you might have today. I'm Detective Feldmann, and this is my friend, Amelia. I'd sure appreciate it if you would let us in and answer some questions."

Simon gawks at me and looks even more dubious. "Um, okaaaaay . . . Come inside."

"That would be great," Isaac says. "If you don't mind."

Simon shrugs and retreats into the house, leaving the door open for us to follow. I pull it shut gently, doubting that we'll need to get out of here urgently. From what I've seen so far of Simon, it seems like he's more motivated to drink Mountain Dew and play Call of Duty rather than kidnap a girl and take a bunch of pictures to send her parents and demand ransom. Seems like too much work for him.

The lack of furniture forces me to politely sit on an ottoman. Simon gestures for Isaac to take the recliner and he takes the gaming chair. I look around the room, searching for clues that show that Simon went through something traumatic in his childhood that might be manifesting in his young adulthood.

There are no pictures on the wall, though I can understand that if your biological father is a psychotic killer. Maybe that's something you don't want to remember every day. In the living room, there is a big-screen TV and about five different gaming consoles lined up in a row, like an army. There's a plastic patio table in the corner of the room, stacked high with Coke cans and empty Chinese food containers.

Before Isaac is even able to begin questioning him, Simon begins the conversation, surprisingly intuitive. "So, I guess you're here about that missing girl," he says.

Isaac tries to hide his surprise at the balls on this kid. He could be the main suspect in this case, and he just saunters into the conversation, come what may. "That's right," Isaac says. "I'll just get on with it then, if you're comfortable talking without a lawyer."

"What do I need a lawyer for if I didn't do nothing wrong?"

"I didn't say you did," Isaac says, drawing out his pad of paper and pen. "I just want to make sure we have all the bases covered. So, did you know her?"

"No," he replies, giving Isaac an odd look. "How would I know her?"

"Just checking," Isaac says. "Do you remember where you were on Thursday around 6 PM?"

"You're looking at it," Simon says, nodding at the gaming setup.

"Can anyone verify that for you?" Isaac asks cordially. I've seen his good cop, bad cop routine, but it's usually him playing both roles. Good cop at first. Bad cop if he doesn't get what he wants.

"Nope," Simon says. "I don't really have many friends."

"Any girlfriend?"

"Nope. Had one for a while, but she cheated on me and I cut her loose."

"And what do you mean by that?"

"I broke up with her. What do you mean, what do I mean by that?"

"Just clarifying." Simon says. "Can you tell us a little about that?"

"What does this have to do with the investigation for the Bridget girl?"

Isaac and I exchange a look. We didn't mention her by name, but he was quick to say it. Maybe it's just because it's been in the news, but it seems unusual that he would call her by name. I can tell Isaac is feeling the same way, because he hones in on it during the next question.

"So you've been following the case pretty closely," Isaac says. "Watching it on TV?"

Simon smiles then, a creepy little grin. "There was a press conference with her parents on earlier. Apparently the kidnapper sent pictures."

Isaac frowns. "Are you sure you don't know anything about this?"

Simon pauses. "I mean, I could make up some stuff if you want. I bet you'd like it if I told you all about my dad, too. Wanna hear about the things he used to do to me? What he did to those women? I guess you already know."

He looks at me pointedly.

It's my turn to shine.

"Simon, I am so glad to see you're in a better place now that your father's behind bars. It must have been so scary for you, seeing what he did."

Simon stares down at his hands, and I notice a scar around his wrist. He must feel me looking at it because he pulls his sleeves down over his hands, as if he's cold.

"What's that?" I ask gently.

"Nothing," he says, avoiding my gaze, and it breaks my heart. He's just a little boy inside. He never got the chance to play carefree. He was always protecting himself from his own father. When I wrote my book, Simon was only about fifteen, but he seemed to be burdened by a load too heavy for anyone to shoulder. He saw things no one should ever see. I just wished I could wrap my arms around and tell him everything was going to be alright.

Maybe that's the tack I should take. Empathy, compassion. Isn't that always the way?

I get off the ottoman and crawl on the floor until I'm sitting right by Simon. I put my hand on his back. I take his arm and push up the sleeve, exposing a deep scar. He grimaces and then looks at me. I can tell he's not used to anyone taking inventory of his pain.

"What happened?" I ask.

He pulls his hand back and sniffles. I realize that he's crying.

"My dad . . ." he begins. "When my mom went to go visit her family, my dad . . ."

"What did he do to you?" I nudge him.

"He used to handcuff me to the toilet. He'd set out some crackers and water for me and then attach me to the toilet so I couldn't get away. Also, he wouldn't have any mess to clean up. That way, he could go out hunting and not worry about me running and telling the police about the ladies he brought home in the middle of the night."

"I'm sorry," I say.

"After my dad got put away, I didn't know if he would stay in jail. Maybe they would let him out. He was good at talking people into things like that."

I sigh. "He's never getting out. I promise."

"One more thing, Simon," Isaac cuts in. "Do you happen to have a basement? I couldn't tell from the outside."

"Nope," Simon replied. "If there's a tornado, I'm basically fucked."

Isaac nods, taking his little notepad and stuffing it in his shirt pocket. Whatever we came here looking for, we didn't find it.

CHAPTER

53

Beyond the Glass

(A. Child, 2019, pp. 156–157)

GERALD SHAPIRO DIDN'T let being a father stop his fun. His wife often left Simon at home to go visit her relatives a couple of states away, and that's when Gerald began to track women through a neighborhood app. He was friendly, he was charismatic, he was still handsome.

He'd pick up one girl, date her for a few weeks, and then drop her like garbage on trash day. This was all by day. By night, he was talking up prostitutes at the gas stations off I-80. No one missed them, and so he made a habit of picking them up, taking them home, assaulting them, and strangling them. All while poor Simon was locked in the bathroom upstairs, plugging his ears to drown out the screams.

One day, Gerald forgot to lock him up. Simon lay terrified in his bed, listening to the screams. The noises from the basement had become so horrific that Simon peed in his pants, but he told himself he was being a baby and tiptoed downstairs to get some dry pajamas out of the dryer. Gerald was down there, and Simon was terrified of disturbing him. But the noises from the basement stopped and the door cre-e-e-e-e-aked open.

Simon was frozen in the darkness, a narrow beam of moonlight illuminating his bare feet. He thought that maybe if he just didn't move, Gerald would overlook him. But when Gerald stomped up the stairs to find out what was going on, he flipped on the lights and saw his son standing there in wet pajamas.

"You little idiot," he said and then grabbed Simon by the ear, pulling him through the kitchen, to the back door. "If you're going to piss yourself, you're going to stay with the dog. You can piss and shit all you want outside. And you'd better stay out there all night, because I'm going to be out here first thing and if you're gone . . ."

Gerald didn't have to finish his thought. The implied threat was awful enough.

Simon spent that night in the doghouse curled up against their terrier, finding comfort in his matted but soft fur. That night, he dreamed of dying, of going up to heaven and meeting all the family members who had died before his time or were just completely alienated because of Gerald's insanity. In his dream, he was loved.

But then the morning came, and out came Gerald, wearing the same clothes he'd worn the night before. The only difference was that these were covered in blood, from the neckline of his shirt, down to the frayed bottom of his pants.

Simon recoiled when Gerald grabbed him by his shirt. He yanked his son out into the cold air and told him to go in and get showered and dressed so he could make Gerald breakfast. He said if Simon ever told his mother what happened when she was gone, he'd kill them both.

That was Simon's life, and I tell this story to show all of the women out there, online, watching media about Gerald's court trial and thinking he's so dreamy. Does this change your opinion of him? And if not, shouldn't it?

CHAPTER 54

Gabby

Iowa City, 2024

Easton and I are sitting on my mother's old bed, facing one another, the computer between us. His nervous habit is on full display as he nibbles his fingernails down to nubs. We've just finished messaging the copycat, who has confessed to getting in over his head. He said he had a situation that he needed help with, and I assured him, as Gerald, that there was someone who would be able to assist him—that "person" being us, of course.

It was strange, how he came so close to naming Bridget as the girl he was having trouble with, but even in his distress he didn't cross that line. Everything he said was very cryptic, but he suggested that he was having problems and he wasn't sure how to get control of the situation. He's got Bridget, and now he doesn't know what to do with her.

It's definitely not enough to go to the cops with, but it's enough to confirm my suspicions. My idea is to go to the cafe where we've arranged to meet him, scout him out from afar, and then follow him, make sure he's driving the black truck and everything. Get his address, call the cops, the end. It seems simple in my mind, wanting to clarify that we are turning in the right person, but at the same time, I want to see for myself that it isn't my father before involving the police. Not that I really believe he has anything to do with it. Not really.

Easton, understandably, is having misgivings. He wanted to call the police before, and now that we're talking about driving out of town to confront a supposed serial killer, he's even further outside of his comfort zone, to put it mildly.

As Easton paces back and forth, I try to reason with him.

"Come on, babe, we won't be in any danger. We'll be in a public place, for goodness' sake. We're just checking things out."

He sighs and runs his hands through his hair. After a long time, he says, "Fine."

I slap my thighs and get up from the bed, anxious to get this show on the road.

"Where are you guys off to?" my grandfather asks when we pass through the living room. He's cozied up with a cooking magazine and a steaming mug of tea.

I've prepared for this. Lifting my backpack up, I say, "Library. We've got a big math test on Monday."

He looks doubtful. "I think you should stay here."

"Come on, Grandpa. As long as I stay with Easton, I'll be fine."

"Well . . ." he grumbles. "Okay. Just be home before dark."

I feel bad, knowing that we probably won't make it back before it's dark, but that's a problem for future me. Present me is worrying that we won't make it in time to meet AnotherChild at the cafe.

"Of course," I say, kissing him on top of his head. "I'll call you if we get held up."

He grunts and nods at Easton, then goes back to his article about how to make the best blueberry muffins. I give Easton a relieved look and rush to the front door before my grandfather can change his mind. Easton hesitates, and I grab the arm of his coat to tug him along.

Outside, we can see our breath coming out in puffs. The weather has dropped a good ten degrees, it seems like, or maybe it's just nerves. We are actually doing this. While my stomach is definitely flip-flopping, I can't deny that I feel exhilarated. As a teenager, you feel like there are so many terrible things happening in the world that you can do nothing about, but this . . . this is something we can do.

We can do this on our own.

We can save Bridget.

We can have justice.

CHAPTER 55

Amelia

I-80, 2024

I stare out the window, my mind running through the conversations we had with Gerald and Simon. Gerald, as always, was completely untrustworthy. I'm not sure whether he had something to do with Bridget's disappearance or not, but I'm fairly sure Simon is in the dark about the whole thing.

The sky darkens, casting an eerie glow over the snowy fields.

I twist my head to look at Isaac's face. He has his eyes solemnly focused on the road and is doing about five over the speed limit. I want to tell him to go faster, that time is of the essence, but if we get into a wreck, we'll be good for nothing.

"Do you believe what Gerald said, that he has nothing to do with Bridget's kidnapping?"

"Yes," Isaac replies. "You don't?"

"I don't know," I say.

I *should* know. After all, I'm the one who spent hours and hours talking with him about his crimes to write my book on him. He's a hard nut to crack, though. I'm sure he's lied to me plenty of times, but I haven't figured out any tell. Sometimes I think *Beyond the Glass* is just a horror story, from Gerald's lips to my pencil, to the minds and imaginations of millions of people. But then there's a matter of eighteen bodies, unexplained if Gerald is innocent.

"He has no reason to lie," Isaac says. "He's going to be behind bars a million years, whether he confesses to hooking up with some other criminal to create this resurgence of his popularity or not. That brings me to my next point. If he had anything to do with it, he definitely would have told us. He's a narcissist. He'll take any attention he can get."

"And Simon?"

"Simon's a fetus," Isaac says. "I can't see him being motivated to get out of bed in the morning, much less kidnap a girl and hold her for ransom."

He reaches over and rubs my neck with his thumb. It's almost enough to distract me, but I can't let this go. I doubt I'll be able to until Bridget is safe in her bed.

I scroll through the pictures the kidnapper released of Bridget. She looks so small, so broken. Streaked with dirt and blood. It could so easily have been Gabby. When I find whoever is behind this, I'm going to see that they go to prison for life. I don't care if it takes the biggest, baddest lawyer. I'll raise money for her parents and help them get the justice they deserve.

"So if it's not Gerald and it's not Simon, who could it be?"

Isaac releases a long breath. "It could be anyone, couldn't it? Any one of his fans who are obsessed with him. That website? I think we should check it out again. Go through it with a fine-toothed comb."

I consider his suggestion and how likely it would be to find the fan who is psychotic enough to copy Gerald's crimes, and my headache comes back.

CHAPTER 56

The Kidnapper

Homestead, 2024

My phone buzzes again.

I don't need to look to see who it is. Renee has been calling me nonstop, and it doesn't take a genius to guess that she's seen the news. Not only have I disobeyed her very direct order to kill the girl, but I've taken pictures of her in our very basement, and they are now being analyzed by every armchair detective with a shred of curiosity and Internet access.

Wincing, I pick up the phone and see that she's texted me.
Pick up the goddamn phone, you fucking idiot.

Sighing, I hit the answer button and hold my phone a few inches away from my ear, preparing for the shriek that is no doubt coming.

"Jared? Jared? Are you there?"

She's not yelling, so I allow myself to press the phone against my ear. "Yes?"

Then she screams. "You idiot! What were you thinking?"

Her voice slices off a piece of my heart. I've heard Renee angry before, but nothing like this. What was I thinking? About us. Everything I do is for us. And for her to say that I'm an idiot for trying to secure money for our future breaks my damn heart.

"Look, I was thinking about our future."

"What about spending our lives in prison appeals to you? Tell me that."

In that moment, I become determined to remedy my mistake as soon as possible. I don't want to tell Renee about my plans to meet with Gerald's friend, though. I need to show that I can step it up and take care of things my way.

"I'll fix it," I say simply and hang up on her. She won't like it, but I'm not going down this road with her. The next time we talk, I'll have solved all our problems and we will be free to do whatever we want. Still, I can't keep my hands from shaking when I reach over and grab for my beer. I take a swig, nervous about what I have to do tonight.

CHAPTER 57

Amelia

Iowa City, 2024

WHEN I GET to Jack's house, no one is there. A panicked phone call to Jack reveals that Gabby went to my father's house to stay the night, which is bizarre because she hasn't seen my father in years. Jack says he'd come to meet me there, but he's at the hospital with Julia right now. Exasperated, I throw my hands in the air and resign myself to seeing my father again.

After Isaac drives me to his place, I find myself standing on the front porch of the house where I grew up. I bang on the door. "Dad!"

He barely opens the door when I demand, "Where is she?"

My father gives me a miserable look. "She went out with her friend, Easton. She promised me she'd be home by now."

"How could you just let her wander away?" I yell at my father. "In the middle of a crisis like this? There's a girl missing, and you just let her go out into a world where a psycho could snatch her and put her through the atrocities Gerald Shapiro was capable of?"

Then I realize I should be directing these accusations at myself. I've been so wrapped up in the search for Bridget, desperate to find the kidnapper before he kills her, that I've neglected my own daughter. The epiphany strikes me like a ton of bricks, and I lean over, hyperventilating.

Isaac puts his hand on my back.

"We'll go out and find her," he says. "She can't have gone far. Let's look at the room she was sleeping in. Maybe we'll find a clue to her whereabouts."

I bite my lip and nod, turning to the direction of my old bedroom. When we get there, I stop and stare. Everything is the way I left it when my father and I had that falling out about me telling my mother's story in *Beyond the Glass*. He said I was ruining her memory, that she didn't deserve her life and death to be published for everyone to see. He said I didn't love her.

I walk into the middle of the room, feeling like I've been caught in a time warp. My posters on the walls, my closet full of clothes, my old TV . . . everything is the same.

Gabby's laptop is open on the bed, her screen saver of a butterfly flitting around on the screen. I sit down and run my fingers along the trackpad, and the last website she was on pops up. It's Google Maps, and the address shown belongs to a cafe in Williamsburg.

"What's this?" I demand.

I navigate away from the map and find her search history. My mouth goes dry. It's that weird Free Gerry website that posts bizarre shit about me all the time. I scan the forum thread, hands flying to my mouth as I see the message from the prison guard and AnotherChild's response. There's a little red number one at the top of the screen, and I click on it. It's a message from AnotherChild to a persona that Gabby must have made up, TomsBoy1. When I read the exchange between them, I scream.

Isaac is right behind me. "Do you have Easton's telephone number?"

"I don't think so," I say, pulling up my contacts and looking, but there's nothing under "Easton." I never thought to get his number. Stupid. So stupid.

"We have to go. Right now." I frantically grab Isaac by the sleeve.

He looks at me. "I think you should stay here in case she comes back."

"No!" I shriek. "I'm coming with you!"

My father clears his throat. He's standing in the doorway. "If Amelia says she's going, there's no stopping her." His voice is grudging. I know he's not happy with me, but he knows me well enough to try to keep me from doing what I decide needs to be done.

"Come on," Isaac says. "You've hardly slept, Amelia."

"No," I insist. "I'm finished talking about this. Let's go."

He holds up his hands, like there's nothing more he can do. I follow him outside and climb into the car. As we pull away, I feel like vomiting.

The helpless feeling in my stomach is reminiscent of when I watched Gerald's trial and couldn't help thinking of the way my mother died.

Like my heart has been shattered.

CHAPTER 58

Beyond the Glass

(A. Child, 2019, pp. 201–202)

I WAS DRESSED IN my nicest clothes. My father insisted. Reporters from all over the world would be at Gerald Shapiro's trial. My dad wanted to make sure I was presentable, even though I couldn't care less how I looked to the rest of the world. It was just easiest to put on the clothes he laid out for me. I felt like I was sleepwalking as we climbed the steps to the courthouse.

The place was packed. After all, his crimes affected many, far and wide. There were mothers and children crying, men with their chests puffed out, just waiting to get a look at the monster who'd robbed us of our loved ones.

We were the lucky ones—or the unlucky ones, depending on how you thought of it—getting a seat in front, better to stare at the face of evil. My father held my hand, and I looked at the ground. To see Gerald's face would be to draw me back to the day, the one where my life was turned upside down.

I looked up as the prosecuting attorney projected pictures of my mother for the judge and jury. There were a couple of her when she was younger. There was one of her holding me, sitting on the edge of a pool, me wearing water wings.

But then the pictures turned savage. She was lying on the ground amongst a million leaves, all red and brown and orange. Her eyes were unseeing, turned up toward the sky. Her shirt had been ripped, and there were dark black-and-blue marks around her neck. I kept my eyes trained downward after that.

Gerald Shapiro's testimony was even worse. He described the lovely woman he met online, musing about her family, comforting him when he told her of his fictional troubles. He had groomed her by saying he had lost his wife, just as she had lost her pregnancy. She let down her guard and went with him to supposedly visit his dead wife's grave.

There he raped her. He killed her. He left her there, like garbage.

I looked at the jury, who appeared to be just as horrified as I was. That was the only consolation, that they were on our side and that Gerald would never, ever get off on these charges. There was one woman in particular who stared at me for almost the whole trial. I wondered if she lost someone, too, if she knew the pain I was feeling. When she saw me looking at her, she raised her hand in a half wave.

She looked a little like my mom.

CHAPTER

59

Gabby

Williamsburg, 2024

WE PARK SEVERAL streets away from the cafe we told AnotherChild we'd meet him at. The area is peppered with hip restaurants and witchy little shops. There are people everywhere I look, despite the cold weather. I suppose Christmas is coming up, a perfect day to get some coffee and do a little shopping. We pass couples holding hands, families smiling at each other, teenagers having snowball fights. It's hard to believe that such an evil presence could exist here, in the midst of the holiday cheer.

When the cafe is in sight, we slow down and look for a place where we can sit to scout out the area. I was hoping we'd get here early and be able to study every person going in, but our disagreement meant we'd taken a while to get on the road, and I fear AnotherChild is already here, somewhere.

We find a bench outside. From our vantage point, we can see inside. It's crowded, almost all of the tables taken and a line at the counter snaking almost to the door. Most of the people are in groups or couples, though. There are only a few people sitting by themselves. One is a woman sitting near the window, an open novel in front of her, along with a mug of coffee and a muffin. A few feet away, an elderly man in a plaid shirt eats a plate full of eggs. My eyes linger on him for a bit longer, but I doubt that a man that old would be able to overpower Bridget.

And then I see him, sitting in the back corner. He has dark hair, grown long, and has sideburns. He looks like he's about thirty years old, but maybe his frown and shifty eyes make him look older to me. There's a plate with a hamburger and fries on the table before him, but he doesn't touch them, only drinks from a bottle of beer as he waits. He keeps looking at the door, like he's expecting someone to come in. I thank goodness that he's probably looking for another man, like him, to help him clean up his mess. He'd never guess that a couple of teenagers pulled one over on him.

Even though I don't think he's noticed us, Easton puts his hand on my arm and gently presses it. "Not so obvious," he says. "We can't afford to screw this up."

I look up and down the street for the black truck, but most of the cars are SUVs or little hybrid cars—only one pickup, and it's red.

"He must have parked on a side street," I say. "We'll have to follow him out."

"I don't like this," Easton says. "Not at all. It's not too late to call the cops."

"And tell them what? That we think some rando in a cafe is Bridget's kidnapper? Based on a couple of messages from a troll on a creepy website?" I'm tired of fighting Easton on this. "If you don't like it, you should just go."

"And leave you here?" he asks, horrified. "I don't think so."

"Then just go with it," I say. "We'll call them as soon as we know for sure."

He is quiet then, and we sit holding hands, taking turns watching the man and pretending to be on our phones so we don't look too suspicious. The man is on his phone, too, probably checking the website for new messages. I suppose I could send one, but I wish he'd just get on with it and leave the cafe so we can follow him home.

Finally, he gets up, digs in his wallet for a credit card, and lets the waitress ring him up at the counter, leaving his beer bottle and an untouched plate for the waitress to clean up. He shrugs on his coat and comes toward us, heading for the exit.

When the man opens the door, I wrap my arms around Easton and lean in for a kiss. He must get the idea because he nuzzles against me, the bristles on his chin tickling my face. The whole time, I keep my eyes on the guy who is now walking away.

We were right. He didn't park on this street. He turns the corner instead. I jump to my feet. "Go get the car!" I squeal at Easton. "We can't lose him!"

I turn to follow the man.

"Let me," Easton says, pressing the keys into my hand. "I'll stall him."

Without stopping to fight with him, I nod and start running away, toward the street where we parked Easton's car. I dodge people every few yards, and it's taking too long, much too long, but finally I make it there. I jump behind the steering wheel and jam the keys into the ignition, turning them to the right, and the engine roars to life.

I speed toward the street I saw Easton disappear down. When I turn the corner, I breathe a sigh of relief when I see that the black truck is still there. But I can't see Easton. Not at first. Then, as the truck pulls away, I realize there are two people sitting in the front.

Easton has gone with him.

I don't even have a license yet, but I'm driving Easton's car like a madwoman, trying to keep up with the strange man as he swerves from lane to lane throughout the dark night. It has started to snow—big, fat flakes that plop onto the windshield before they get scraped away by the wipers. We wind our way out of the city and the suburbs until the houses become farther and farther apart and soon disappear altogether.

The needle showing the gas tank drops lower and lower, and I watch in terror as it gets closer to empty. Just when I think I'm going to be stranded on the road in the middle of nowhere, the pickup turns onto a gravel road. I slow down, letting the truck disappear over a hill before I follow him. I turn off the lights, and I am guided by the moonlight as we finish our last mile. I see his taillights turn, and he pulls up beside an old house. A porch that is half falling apart runs along the front of the house, and I see light glowing from a partial window on the side of the house, very low, as though it overlooks a basement.

I stall in the road, waiting for the man to turn off his car and go inside, although I'm gripped by terror that Easton is going to go into the house with him. What was he thinking? I frantically search my purse for my phone before I realize it's still at the police station.

We are out here alone.

I watch as the two of them slam the doors to the pickup and go inside. At least the man isn't overpowering Easton. He's not at gunpoint. He wouldn't go inside unless he was fairly sure that he could keep himself safe. From the way the man was swerving on the road, I'm guessing he's fairly intoxicated. He must have been drunk when he entered the cafe. At least Easton has his wits about him.

When the two disappear and the front door slams behind them, I park at the edge of the property, switching off the engine and climbing out. There's no doubt in my mind that I have to go inside, to make sure Easton is okay. But I have to be careful, silent, not let the man know I'm there at all.

I close the car door with a gentle click and trudge up toward the house, clutching my keys in my hand like they showed me in a self-defense class my mom made me take. I wish I had a gun, not that I would know how to use it. Or anything, really, something sharp or heavy. These keys are not going to hold up if I get into a real showdown with Gerald's copycat.

The lights are on inside the house now, and through the curtains I see the two standing and talking. I can see Easton's face. He looks very serious, nodding, as though listening intently to whatever the kidnapper is saying. I have no doubt in my mind now that the man is the one who took Bridget. The truck, the house with a basement, it's all coming together in my mind.

I don't like this. Not one bit.

I think of the game "ding dong ditch" that Easton and I used to play, where we would creep up on a house, ring the doorbell, and then run away. I am tempted to do just that so it will distract the kidnapper and Easton can sneak away.

But then Bridget will be left there, all alone.

I'm about to say the hell with it and break into the house to find Bridget myself when someone tackles me from behind. They don't speak, just grab my arm and twist it around my back.

"Ow!" I say, startled, and then a soft rag is pressed over my mouth, stinking of something fruity, like cherries.

That's the last thing I know before I am swept into darkness.

CHAPTER 60

Beyond the Glass

(A. Child, 2019, pp. 144–145)

IN THE INFANCY of Gerald Shapiro's murderous career, he used his charm to woo ladies and get them to follow him to the place of their imminent demise. But as he grew older, his age got in the way of him securing the type of woman he wanted to defile—namely, young, pretty targets. He had to up his game, and he did that with anesthetic chloroform. He'd seen it used in a movie once to knock out a woman police officer. The villain dipped a handkerchief in chloroform, and as he held it against the woman's mouth and nose, she lost consciousness.

Gerald says he was nervous, using this new concoction. He wasn't sure at first if it would work, so he tried it on himself and fell onto his bed, passed out for about an hour. His head ached when he came to, but he was elated because he knew that this was the key to what he wanted.

He first used it on a young woman who'd been out on a date and was returning to her home in the early evening hours. It was dark enough for him to approach her without being noticed, and he grabbed her and pressed the handkerchief to her mouth. Somehow, he didn't get a tight enough grip, and she escaped and ran into her house, locking the doors behind her. He slipped away in the night, letting her go, but that didn't keep him down.

The next time he tried it, he hid in a park early in the morning before the sun had come up. He'd scouted the place beforehand to check out the runners who liked to get their workout done before the sunrise. His interest was piqued by a runner with long red hair swept back in a ponytail. She was usually listening to a Walkman, so he'd be able to sneak up on her without being heard.

He selected a Friday morning to catch his prey, but the red-haired runner did not show up that day. Angry, he decided to go after the next best thing and assaulted a random woman who was going for a brisk morning walk. She wasn't to his taste, he said—too old, too heavy, but he took what he could get. The chloroform worked this time. The woman was found on the same trail the next day, her lips smeared with lipstick and garish blue eye shadow painted on her eyes. She'd been strangled. That's what Gerald was known for, strangling his victims, making up their faces, and taking pictures. The woman didn't really fit his profile, but the police attributed the killing to him nonetheless.

Up until the day he was caught, this was his new form of knocking out prospective victims. It was relatively cheap, could be ordered online, and was extremely effective when used correctly. It was perfect for his purposes.

CHAPTER

61

Amelia

I-80, 2024

THE HEATER IN Isaac's truck is blasting, and I unzip my jacket, gasping for fresh air. Even though he is driving seventy-five miles an hour, it feels as though we are crawling, and the miles between here and Williamsburg seem endless.

"She has a fire in her belly, that one," Isaac says, trying to distract me. "Reminds me of someone else I know." He squeezes my hand.

"I should have been there," I lament.

If I hadn't gone with Isaac, I'd have been there to stop Gabby from pulling her stupid little prank—granted, it was one that uncovered where the kidnapper is, I have a terrible feeling. If anything happens to her, I will never forgive myself.

"Even if your father had forbidden her from going, she would have found a way to sneak out," Isaac says, reading my mind. "You, of all people, must know that."

"I think I know my daughter better than you."

"She's not stupid," Isaac says. "She was probably just checking things out. She'll call us when she knows for sure."

I shake my head. "I just don't know."

Using Isaac's phone as a hot spot, I take out Gabby's laptop and look it over. The cafe on Google Maps pops up, and my stomach seethes like there are a dozen snakes in it. Isaac called the local police to go there and look for Gabby, but she wasn't there, and the workers hadn't seen anyone with her description.

I take a deep breath and look back at the other open tabs. There's the fake profile that she created. I click on the messages and review them. I try sending the kidnapper a message saying hello just to see if he's online, but my message goes unread. He's somewhere else, doing God knows what, and awful things plague my mind. I picture my daughter lifeless in the stream that girl was found in last week—or locked in a basement, facing horrors like Gerald described when I was writing my book. I know what Gerald is capable of, and if this copycat is even half as bad, we're all in a lot of fucking trouble.

Isaac's cell phone rings. He picks it up, staring straight ahead, at the snow that's piling up on the road before us. "Yes?" He listens for a minute or so. "I see. I can't come in right now, but I'll be there when I can." He pauses. "I don't know. A few hours, maybe."

"What is it?" I can hear the panic in my own voice.

He takes a deep breath. "There's been some news."

"What?" I'm shaking.

"Your husband's girlfriend, Julia? She called the station."

"I'm not following. Why?"

I remember the teachers who said Bridget left Jack's classroom crying just last week. Could he actually be involved?

"She was going through Jack's phone, she said, looking for pictures of the ultrasound they had taken a few weeks ago. She found photos, Amelia. I'm so sorry to tell you this. But they're of Bridget."

Suddenly, I can't breathe. I think about how young Julia was when he first started seeing her, not much older than Bridget. So maybe there's some truth to it, maybe he was carrying on with her. But he'd never hurt her. There's no way.

"They were taken in a basement, she said. He had her chained up, and she—" His voice breaks then, but then he gets it together. "It looked like she was dead. Julia was able to get away from Jack, and the police are looking for him now."

Vomit rises in my throat. I scramble for the door handle, and Isaac steps on the brakes. A car bangs on their horn and swerves around us. We pull to a stop, and I'm barely able to make it outside before I heave my guts out.

Could it be true? Is this who Jack was all along, and I was just too blind to see it? He always made fun of those true crime guys who spend hours on Reddit, discussing unsolved murders. And here he is, turning out to be a kidnapper and a killer.

It all comes back to me. How he was the first person to contact me after Bridget had been kidnapped. How he was reluctant to take Gabby for the weekend, though normally he loves to have her. The long hours he spent at school grading papers, according to Gabby. Maybe he was doing something else. Maybe he was with Bridget.

But there's just one thing that doesn't make sense.

Why would he take her to Williamsburg?

CHAPTER

62

The Kidnapper

Homestead, 2024

I can't get over how young the kid looks, although he has reassured me several times that he's twenty years old and that he gets mistaken for being a teenager all the time. I guess it shouldn't surprise me. If Gerald were going to mentor someone, they would have to be inexperienced, impressionable. That way he could mold them into the man he once was. It sends a bolt of jealousy through me, but I push it down in order to focus on the task at hand.

To get rid of the girl.

I belch.

Too many beers before our meeting. I had a couple before even leaving the house and then just kept drinking on the way to the cafe. It was the only thing I could think of, to push away the uneasiness of the girl still being in my basement and the cops liable to show up at my door at any moment. Or, even worse than the cops, Renee . . .

TomsBoy1 has promised to help me with all that, though. He said he's been helping Gerald from the outside for almost two years now. I wasn't the only one following in his footsteps. There've been a couple before me, guys he met through the website, and Tom's Boy, as I've started to refer to him in my head, has helped them to erase their involvement from the murders completely. The first thing I needed to do was bring him to my house—to where the girl is—so he can assess the situation and figure out what to do next.

"You want a beer?" I ask him. The absurd thought runs through my mind that he's not old enough to drink yet, but then I realize where we are and what we're about to do and figure I might as well offer him one. The kid looks nervous but finally takes me up on the offer.

I stagger into the kitchen and throw open the door, finding the rest of the case right where I left it. Renee wouldn't be pleased if she were here. She's warned me about drinking when I'm doing my thing, but the thing is that I can't help it sometimes and need something to calm my nerves.

After fishing out a couple of brewskis, I turn around and go back into the living room . . . only to freeze in my tracks. Tom's Boy looks terrified, and when I see why, I go numb. Renee is standing in front of the door, the lax body of a girl at her feet.

When I look closer, I realize who it is.

The cross necklace. Just as Gerald had described.

"Gabrielle," I say, feeling suddenly very sober.

I'm not sure where to begin. Where did she come from? How did Renee find her? But before I ask her anything, Renee bursts into an angry tirade.

"Huh? Is that all you have to say for yourself? You were supposed to be fixing this. And I come home to find you drinking beers with some kid while she's prowling around the house? How stupid are you?" She practically spits the words.

Tom's Boy has gone over to the girl, leaning over her, and I realize he's not who he said at all. Somehow, together, these two tricked me. I don't know how they figured out who I was, but they got me to share my location, which means . . . which means the cops can't be far behind.

CHAPTER

63

Amelia

Williamsburg, 2024

It's strange where your mind goes when you're in full panic mode. As we close in on Williamsburg, I think about the day Gabby was born. It was a day of contradictions. May third, but it was snowing. Jack was convinced she would be a boy, but she turned out to be... well, Gabby. We thought first babies took forever to deliver, but everything happened so fast.

One minute I was standing in the kitchen making waffles; the next thing I knew, my water broke and my calves and feet were drenched. Because I was so excited, I'd had my bags packed since the beginning of the first trimester. So all we had to do was grab them and head out the door.

The doctor got into a fender bender on the way to the hospital, so the nurses ended up delivering Gabby. We named her after Nurse Gabrielle, the first person in the whole entire world to hold Gabby in her arms.

Once Gabby was cleaned off, they passed her to me. She looked like a cross between a clown and a little alien, with gigantic blue eyes and tufts of dark hair sprouting haphazardly around her scalp.

She was beautiful.

I've never felt a connection like that before and never since. She cried, and it felt like I was dying inside. She breastfed like a champ from the very first time.

She was my heart.

She *is* my heart.

How could I even entertain the idea of letting her read that book? How could I let her get mixed up in all of this? I've been Gerald Shapiro's main contact for the past ten years. I know how he operates, and I'm sure his copycat will do the same.

Kidnap her, torture her, kill her.

My stomach is in knots. There are two trucks in front of us driving side by side at an excruciatingly slow pace. Isaac lays on the horn, but they continue hogging the interstate, and it's killing me. Finally, finally we make it to Williamsburg, and Isaac parks in front of the cafe with his lights on.

I run inside, even though I know she won't be there, because that's what the police told us when they searched the cafe. There are still some of them there, chatting with the service staff. One sees Isaac and comes over to talk to us. But I leave them, looking everywhere, under tables, behind the bar, in the women's bathroom.

I even barge into the men's bathroom to see if she could be in there. A large man with a beer belly stands there, shielding himself with his hand. "Damn, lady, what's your problem?"

Crazy with fear, I can't stop myself from crying, wailing my daughter's name. Isaac has to come in to retrieve me, steering me toward the other police officers standing near the front door.

"So she's not here," Isaac says. "What's the next step?"

One of the other police officers said, "Does she have her phone? We can trace it. Of course, that'll take a little time."

"No, it's at the police station in Iowa City."

The police officer nods. "The waitress said there was a man here earlier who didn't eat any of his food. He seemed very anxious. We think it could be the kidnapper. He used a card to pay for his meal. We're tracing it right now to find his address."

I nod, feeling sick.

Turning to Isaac, I say, "Do you think Jack has her? It couldn't be him. Otherwise, the police would have recognized his name on the bill. Unless he's using someone else's credit card."

He stares at me for a moment. "Do you have a picture of him on your phone?"

"Of course." I dig my phone out my purse and find a picture of Jack at Gabby's last birthday and hand it to Isaac, who takes it over to the counter and speaks to a couple of waitresses who are standing there, looking very upset. I watch as he flashes the phone to the women, and when they shake their heads, I feel relief mixed with confusion.

It's not Jack.

But then how did he have pictures of Bridget on his phone?

The whole thing is driving me insane.

Isaac is back at my side. "Everything is going to be okay, Amelia."

When the police officer we were talking to before comes over with a little piece of paper with an address scribbled on it, I snatch it up and pull Isaac toward the exit. "Let's go."

He hesitates. "We should wait for the other police officers."

"No," I hiss. "We have to go now."

Isaac nods. He knows there's no use in arguing.

CHAPTER 64

Gabby

Homestead, 2024

When I come to, my head aches. I touch it gingerly. I open my eyes, expecting to be in my room. What I see instead is a blurry room, the walls lined with insulation. I am lying on a mattress with a cool hand on my forehead. Someone is touching me, watching me. I swivel my head to catch sight of the person, expecting the worst. But, even with my wonky vision, it's like looking in a mirror—the long, dark hair and blue eyes. And that's when it all comes together, getting grabbed from behind, a rag smelling like cherries pressed to my nose and mouth. And she—the other prisoner in this basement—is Bridget.

Hope surges through my veins when I see her. She's still alive, which means the kidnapper mimicking Gerald is taking his time. Easton will figure out how to get in touch with my mom. Unless something terrible has happened to him. I try to sit up, but my head swims, and I have to lie back down for a minute.

When my vision clears, I see that Bridget has a doomed look on her face. She reaches out a hand to me, touches my hair. "Did he snatch you, too?"

I sit up and nod. "I was in the yard, waiting for Easton, and someone knocked me out and brought me here."

None of this looks like it surprises Bridget. The light has gone out of her. She drops her hand and pulls herself into a little ball beside me.

"They won't find us. That's what he said, and everything he's said has come true so far. You might as well accept it now."

"Who's he?" I demand, praying she doesn't say my father.

"He's been wearing a mask," she says. "But he has terrible eyes. I was able to see those."

She would have heard my father's voice when she was in his class, and thankfully she doesn't mention any familiarity. I decide to carefully ask her about the yearbook with her picture scribbled in it and why she was crying in his classroom before she disappeared. Dread pools at the bottom of my stomach.

I want to know, but I don't.

"Can I ask you something?" I say, testing the waters. Bridget has stood up and is agitated, fluttering around the room. I'm not sure if she's totally clearheaded, but I have to try.

"Bridget, did you leave a yearbook in my father's classroom?"

She stares through me as if she didn't hear my question.

I snap my fingers in front of her face.

"A yearbook?" she reacts belatedly, blinking her eyes.

"Yeah, did you leave one in my dad's classroom? He had it at his apartment, and I want to know how he found it."

Bridget makes eye contact with me, and it seems like she's going to get it together enough to answer some questions.

"Where did you leave your yearbook?" I ask again.

She shakes her head. "I don't know. I cleaned out my bag and must have misplaced it somewhere. It could have been in your father's room. I don't really remember."

"There was something weird about your yearbook," I say, and I'm not sure how to put the second part tactfully. "Your picture was scribbled out."

She bites her lip. "Yeah, that was Marissa Donahue. I was passing it around to get signatures, and she took the liberty to share what she really thought of me. She's been pissed at me ever since I stood up for myself and didn't let her copy my homework anymore. At least, I'm pretty sure it was her, but I don't have fingerprints or anything . . ." She gave a short laugh. "Sorry, that's just . . . gallows humor, or something."

That makes sense. The whole story seems realistic. I could totally see Marissa doing something like that. She's sort of a bitch sometimes.

"And crying in my father's classroom? Easton said you came out looking all blotchy, like you were upset. What was up with that?"

"I was going through a lot of stuff."

"What kind of stuff?" I ask.

She looks embarrassed. "Family stuff. My mom was super concerned about the stuff I was reading and looking at online, and she thought about pulling me out of public school and homeschooling me. Your dad had been talking about the education system, and I guess I just . . . lost it, a little. He let me stay in his room after class to pull myself together."

"So he didn't come on to you?"

Bridget looks horrified, shakes her head.

A load off my mind. That's putting it mildly.

"So how did you get down here?" she asks.

I tell her that we were looking for her, but I was knocked out cold and brought to the basement. She nods, slowly absorbing the story.

"Easton should be around here somewhere. He came to check the place out. At least, that's what I think he was doing. But . . ." My mind is hazy, and I try to sort through exactly what happened. "He was inside with the kidnapper, but I was outside when I was attacked. There must be two of them."

She shrugs. "It's just been him since I've been here. Although I hear him talking to someone on the phone a lot."

I wonder if Easton is okay. Why wouldn't the kidnappers have brought him down here with us too? I start to get a really bad feeling.

I just wish I could get up and do today over. Have a leisurely breakfast with Grandpa, wait for Mom to get back, and contact Isaac and the police to handle this. How could I be so stupid? It seems like I'm asking that question a lot lately.

CHAPTER 65

Beyond the Glass

(A. Child, 2019, pp. 189–190)

BY THE END, Gerald was tired and slow. It almost seemed that he wanted to get caught. At least, that's what I thought when Isaac and I got access to Sophie Dixon's Facebook account. She was his final victim and the one who led us to him. I think about her all the time; if only we could have seen her account beforehand, we could have warned her.

Besides physically, he hadn't changed so much from when he targeted my mother. He was still looking for vulnerable women, and he found Sophie through a cancer survivor's group. She had just undergone a double mastectomy, and reading her messages with him was excruciating. Her raw pain and desperation to communicate with someone who understood her plight left her open to his message in which he said he'd had testicular cancer and was struggling with the same feelings she was after his orchiectomy. They'd talked for months before she agreed to meet with him in person, this time at a public library.

When questioned about their encounter, Gerald said that she'd been browsing the self-help section with a stack of books that had titles like *After Cancer: What to Do Now*. They sat at a table near the window and talked at length. Gerald was an expert at making women feel beautiful, desirable, and somehow safe. This time he played the game a little longer, arranging another meeting to attend a movie with her the following weekend. Afterward, he asked her to come home with him for a nightcap, and it didn't end well for her.

Isaac and I studied the Facebook account he used for his alias, Orson Buchman. The profile picture was one of him, but it was in black and white, showing only his silhouette. He must have used it for some time before settling on Sophie because it had public posts going back three years, chronicling his fictional disease and his feelings about it. He was friends with over 200 people, most of them women in the Midwest. Sophie seemed to have the unlucky distinction that she lived close enough to him that he could visit with her several times before making the kill. It must have been getting harder for Gerald to corner his prey.

I thought there was no way that he'd still be using the same Facebook account. A seasoned killer such as himself would know that he could be traced. He explained later that he knew it wasn't a good idea, but he couldn't resist checking his messages every once in a while to see if any of his previous targets had contacted him. He'd spent way too much time building up that pool of potential victims.

Isaac got a warrant to get access to the account, and he found that Gerald was still active. We planned a sting operation to apprehend him by inventing a woman much like Sophie. A single cancer survivor living in the Midwest, looking for a connection.

I still remember the night he was arrested. It was in a Des Moines city park, and he was walking toward the merry-go-round carrying a bouquet of daisies. I watched from the car as the police surrounded him, and I *recognized* him as the strange man who attended my mother's funeral years before. The feeling I experienced when he was finally handcuffed and taken away was nothing short of transcendent. It felt like my mother was watching with me, and I was filled with peace, seeing her killer being packed into the back of a police car.

That day, justice was served.

CHAPTER 66

Amelia

Homestead, 2024

The address is along a country road to the north of Williamsburg. It stretches past cornfields in either direction. It has stopped snowing, but the couple of inches on the street out here haven't been plowed yet. This makes it extremely slippery, and, a few times, I'm afraid we're going to go into the ditch, but we don't.

"What are we going to do when we get there?" I ask Isaac.

"Not *we*," he says. "What will *I* do when we get there? I'm going to take care of this motherfucker once and for all."

We keep driving until eventually a farmhouse appears on the horizon.

As we approach, I see that the windows are dark, but there are three cars parked in the front, one of which is Easton's.

Wild scenarios run through my head. I think of all my interviews with Gerald, how he talked about dressing up the girls and doing their makeup before attacking them. I think of my daughter in there, terrified, just wishing someone would come and save her. I'm about to get out of the car and run up to the door myself when Isaac puts his hand on my leg.

"You need to let me take care of this," he says.

It reminds me of the last time we confronted evil, how Isaac took charge and apprehended Gerald in the park that day. Isaac knows what he's doing. I'm overcome by gratitude that he is here. He is calm and collected, and he will take care of this situation.

And if he doesn't, I will.

CHAPTER 67

Beyond the Glass

(A. Child, 2019, pp. 189–190)

I DEMANDED TO BE there when Isaac questioned Gerald. Perhaps it was because Isaac was the boss, maybe because he knew it would mean so much to me personally and also for my professional research, but Isaac said yes. I stood behind the one-way mirror, fighting the urge to cry. I could still recite every word of that conversation from memory.

At first Gerald was coy, answering questions with more questions.

"What were you doing at the park?"

"What do you think I was doing?"

"What were you planning on doing with the woman you were meeting?"

"I think you know the answer to that, don't you?"

It went on for hours, Gerald playing his little game. But Isaac didn't give an inch of leeway. Eventually, he broke Gerald down, and once the dam broke, Gerald was ready to confess everything he did. He knew the jig was up, and he wanted to take credit for the damage he did.

The process of his trial was long and tedious. Everybody who was suspected to be his victim had to be verified, the families getting the closure they'd been waiting on for years. I was there when Isaac called some of the victims' loved ones, and I got secondhand satisfaction, knowing Gerald's reign of terror was over.

CHAPTER

68

Gabby

Homestead, 2024

BRIDGET AND I sit facing each other, our legs crisscrossed, filling each other in on what had happened since Bridget's disappearance. Gerald's copycat is a sicko, but at least he isn't Gerald Shapiro. Otherwise we'd probably be dead already.

I groan and rest my head in my hands.

How is this happening?

That's when we hear the banging on the door upstairs.

Who is that? Could it be Easton? The police?

The both of us sit up straight, shocked into silence for only a moment, and then both of us jump to our feet and start screaming and banging on the walls.

"We're down here!" I yell. "Please help us!"

"Help! Help! Help!" Bridget repeats over and over.

"Wait, shhhhh . . ." I say, making out a voice that is soft but conversational. It's a woman's voice. Maybe a female police officer? A neighbor? It doesn't matter who it is, as long as they can help us get away from the psycho responsible for this.

"No, I'm afraid I haven't seen anyone like that," a woman's voice flutters down the stairs. She sounds cool and gentle, how my mother normally sounds, when she's not thinking about serial killers and kidnappings. "Well, I'm afraid you'll need a warrant for that."

"Did you hear that? It's a woman."

Bridget nods, her eyes wide. "What does that mean?"

"I-I don't know." I can't believe that a woman could have drugged me and hauled me inside, unless she was very strong. Suddenly screaming doesn't seem like the best idea at this point in time. If she's able to send the police away, I'm not sure what to do next. A lot can happen in the length of time it would take them to get a warrant and come back.

We hear the front door close upstairs, and one set of footsteps makes its way through the living room and kitchen and to the door to the basement. I don't know about Bridget, but I'm barely breathing, so sure that the woman will hear me. Of course, she knows we're down here, so that doesn't make any sense. But I'm kind of bargaining with God—*if I'm quiet now, please keep her from coming down here.*

No such luck.

I hear a click as the door is unlocked, and the knob to the door slowly, slowly turns. Bridget and I are both pressed against the wall on the right side of the door, so when she comes down, she won't see us. That might be the only way for us to get out. I nudge Bridget with my toe and motion toward the stairs, miming us knocking the woman over and making a clean getaway.

Her gait is painfully slow, as if she's enjoying torturing us. Finally, finally, she reaches the bottom step . . . and stops. She must be looking at the empty mattress and wondering where we're at. I try to muster up the courage to make a fist and hit her as hard as I can, winning us enough time, but I am frozen with fear.

Then she turns the corner and meets us, face to face.

I gasp.

Standing before us, in a stylish black dress with a red silk scarf and sensible flats, is Julia, my would-be stepmother. She looks like she's dressed up to go to a leisurely brunch, but she's down here in a dingy basement.

What is wrong with this picture?

I am shocked. Maybe she really came with my mother and just got down here first. But then I see the knife in her hand, and I know I'm wrong.

"Julia," I say, my voice a little squeak.

"Surprise," she replies. "And don't call me that. My name is Renee."

Bridget and I have both started backing away from my father's fiancée. It doesn't make any sense. How could this woman who made cookies with me yesterday be threatening me with a knife? The only thing I can think of is that it was me she was after all along. Bridget is just collateral. Suddenly, it becomes clear to me that Julia is the one who tracked us at the coffee shop the other night, maybe using my dad's Life360 app. It was she who left the threat in my mailbox. She's trying to terrorize me.

I only have a few more inches to the woodworking table. It will be a barrier between us. I can grab one of the tools to defend us. It's the best I can do.

Renee grabs Bridget and lunges at her with the knife. Not even thinking, I grab Bridget's other hand and yank her as hard as I can toward the woodworking bench. I push her beneath, but there isn't enough time for me to crawl under as well. I blindly grab a weapon, but in my haste find only a screwdriver.

"*You* kidnapped Bridget?" I ask incredulously.

She rolls her eyes.

"No," she says, "but I'm handling it."

There's a route for me to reach the basement stairs, but I am so thrown off by this development, I feel like my feet are nailed to the floor.

"So . . . if you didn't kidnap Bridget, then who did?"

"Jared!" Renee yells. "Come down here!"

"Who's Jared?"

Julia sighs. "He's my boyfriend. He was supposed to take you that night at the coffee shop, but he got confused because you two look so much alike, so . . ."

"But . . . but why would you want to kidnap me?"

"To get back at your bitch of a mother," she spits. "Since she put away my father."

"What? But . . . according to the book, Gerald only had a son . . ."

"You're so stupid sometimes. A man can have more than one kid. Just because I was born out of wedlock doesn't make it any less true. A bastard can love their father as much as a legitimate child."

There are footsteps coming down the stairs, and I back up into the corner as far as I can. "Please don't hurt me."

But then I see the man coming down the stairs, the one from the cafe in Williamsburg. He is swaying and holding his head with one hand, blood trickling down the side. Someone must have hit him. For a moment, I let myself hope that Easton is alive, was able to get away.

The man grabs the knife from Renee, pausing to touch her belly with his good hand, in a protective gesture. It's so surreal. Is she pregnant with my father's child, or does the baby belong to this man? It's like I'm putting together a puzzle, but there are way too many pieces.

"You're cheating on my dad?" I ask Julia.

She looks bored. "Your dad was only a tool. By getting close to him, I was able to get close to you. I used your dad's phone to get the coordinates to let my man know where you were to grab you. He just made a mistake." She swats her boyfriend's hand away from her stomach. "It was supposed to impress him."

"Impress who? Gerald?" I ask. "He's a serial killer."

Julia glares at me. "Yes, but I guess I want what everyone always wants, to make my father proud of me. See, I know your parents went to interview Simon, that little runt. Gerald doesn't even acknowledge me, although my mom sent him a million letters asking for child support. All I want is his recognition, for him to see me as his daughter."

"The cops were just here," I remind Julia. "If you hurt us, they'll find you here, but if you let us go, I won't say anything."

"Yeah, I think we're safe for now. As long as we get this show on the road. Hon, can we get on with it? I'm feeling sick. I'll go see if that kid has woken up yet. Let me know when you're done." She turns toward the stairs.

The man starts to chase me around the room. I run toward the cot, jump over it, and sprint toward the stairs. He catches me a few inches away from them and yanks me back onto the mattress, slicing wildly.

I can feel the steel enter my arm above my elbow. It feels so cold, so cold it's almost hot. He plunges the knife into me again, this time entering my stomach. I double over in agony. The screwdriver I'd been holding clatters to the floor uselessly. He's about to cut me again, but we hear noises outside. I feel like I might be imagining it, but I think I hear my mother calling my name. I open my mouth back to answer her, but the kidnapper has his hand on my mouth.

I'm not usually one for prayer, but I say one now.

Please, let my mother find me.

Please.

CHAPTER

69

Beyond the Glass

(A. Child, 2019, pp. 226)

THE QUESTION OF Gerald Shapiro's parenthood is murky at best. It is known that he has a son and that their relationship is tepid, but what about other children he might have fathered? He confessed that during his trucking days he had intimate relations with several women who got off safely. Lucky for him, they never talked.

The question remains: Did Shapiro become the way he is because of his genes or because of his environment? If a serial killer begets children, are they likely to become as criminal as he has? There is such a gene called the MAO-A gene, referred to as the "serial killer" or "warrior" gene. Scientists have argued whether the gene is a legitimate cause of aggressive behavior, but the theory has been addressed in multiple trials and has gotten several criminals reduced sentences based on their genetic makeup.

If the studies hold water as time goes on, they may even be able to test for aggression before a child is born, which leads to another can of worms entirely. For now, it is only a factor in Shapiro's situation. His known son was tested and found to have questionable sanity, which is understandable, given his heritage. But there may be other children out there, ironically, struggling because of the life Shapiro has given them.

CHAPTER 70

Amelia

Homestead, 2024

I'M SITTING IN the front of Isaac's truck, wringing my hands as I wait.

Eventually, Isaac comes back to his truck.

Alone.

"Any luck?" I ask, anxiety threading my voice.

"I don't know. It was some woman at the door. She said there was nobody there besides her boyfriend, but I thought I heard someone calling out. Then she started talking really loudly, trying to pull my focus off what might have been happening inside, and she shut the door."

"Can't you go back?" I plead.

"Technically, we need a warrant to go inside, but if I'm afraid there might be imminent bodily harm, I can go in. I might go walk the perimeter of the house, see if I can see anything."

He closes the car door, and I silently slide out and follow Isaac as he approaches the house. He pauses at the porch, listening, but it's quiet, so he circles around to the side, where a small rectangular window peeks out from behind a garden of dead vines and leaves.

I think I hear Gabby's voice and cry out.

Isaac looks behind him and sees me standing there, but there's nothing he can tell me, because he hears the girl too.

"Gabby!" I choke out.

She is in pain, I know it.

And so, I give no credence to the law that says any homeowner can keep my daughter away from me when she needs me. I run around to the front of the house, Isaac close at my heels.

He tries the door, but it's locked. "Hello? Hello? Open up!"

No one responds, so he draws his gun and puts a bullet through the lock.

"Gabby!" I scream, running toward the kitchen.

There is a door that clearly leads to the basement.

Isaac tries, but it's locked.

You know how there are those mothers who can lift up cars when their children are in danger? Imagine that's me, only with a door. I kick as hard as I possibly can, and the whole thing caves inward. The door hangs ajar, revealing a dark staircase.

"Stay here," Isaac warns me. "I'll take care of it."

With that, he takes the stairs two at a time.

I can't believe that he would ask me to stay put, not when my daughter's life is in danger. I tentatively take a few steps down the stairs, my eyes straining against the absence of light. Isaac has reached the bottom and is yelling at someone.

"Drop your weapons!" Isaac screams.

I inch my way closer until I can see what's going on, and my heart stops. A man I've never seen is holding my daughter, who's facing me with a terrified expression on her face. And then I see the blood all over her shirt and feel faint.

"Gabby!"

She hears my voice and looks up, crying. "Mom."

"Let her go!" I yell at the strange man. He looks at me in confusion. There's too much going on. I'm afraid he'll get scared and slit her throat out of panic.

I flash back to the day she was born, covered in blood and screaming, just as she is now. I've only had her for sixteen years. Please, please let us get out of this.

"I told you to stay upstairs," Isaac chastises me.

I do the opposite and race down the rest of the stairs, into the middle of the pandemonium. In the corner, I see Bridget cowering beneath a bench. At least she is safe.

The puddle of blood on the floor, it's too big.

"Please," I beg the man. "Please let her go."

The man with the knife looks at me, then looks back to Isaac, who grunts in frustration. I have just made his life more difficult, upping the possible body count from two to three. But I honestly think the man is listening to me. He loosens his grip imperceptibly, and I think he's about to let my daughter go, but then I hear something behind me.

"I mean it, drop the knife!" Isaac yells.

The man looks uncertain, seeming to focus on something behind me.

"I can't trust you to do anything right."

It hits me just then, who the voice belongs to. A woman I've come to hate, but I would never have imagined that she could be a part of this. Standing behind me is my ex-husband's fiancée, Julia. I spin around and sure enough, it's her.

"Are you going to do it? You coward. You'll never be what Gerald was. You're pitiful, just a fan. I thought you were special, that my dad would be proud of you, that you'd continue his work," Julia spits.

What the hell is she talking about? Her dad? She's Gerald's daughter?

The man clutches at Gabby more tightly, and I call out, feeling her pain as my own. He presses the knife to her throat and begins to cut.

"No!" I scream.

A gunshot.

The man thuds to the ground, leaving Gabby hunched over and shivering. I run to her and wrap her in my arms, eyes closed tightly. "Thank God."

I barely even notice Julia, who is running back up the stairs. Isaac chases her in hot pursuit. At this point, I don't even care. Nothing matters but my daughter. I kneel beside her and try to staunch the blood that is pouring from her stomach.

She is crying onto my shoulder.

"It's going to be okay," I cry. "Just hold on for me, baby. Hold on."

CHAPTER

71

Beyond the Glass

(A. Child, 2019, pp. 230)

OF ALL THE atrocities Gerald committed throughout his reign of terror, the only thing he regretted was getting caught. He bit off more than he could chew, he admitted. He sat in the interrogation room, staring at Isaac confrontationally.

He asked for coffee.
He asked for a candy bar.
He asked for his lawyer.
But at no point did he ask for forgiveness.

Gerald seems completely incapable of experiencing remorse, and this showed after his arrest. He wasn't sorry for hurting those girls. He was only sorry it had to come to an end.

When Gerald's lawyer came, he stopped the interrogation, but we had enough, we had all we needed. We caught him red-handed, and he was going to pay.

CHAPTER 72

Gabby

Iowa City, 2024

WAKING UP IS a process. I first hear the beeping, strong and steady, my heartbeat. Breathing in and out hurts. I can feel where the knife pierced my stomach. Bandages cover the wound, but I can see the blood seeping through them. The same with my arm—layers of gauze squeeze me at the elbow, and I'm unable to roll onto my side. I suspect that the pain would be more vicious if I wasn't on some major pain meds. Woozy and out of it, I feel as though I'm floating above everything.

My mother is there, and I can see the toll the ordeal has taken on her. There are deep, dark circles under her eyes, and the rest of her face is completely pale. She looks as though she's aged twenty years in one day. She takes my hand and rubs it reassuringly.

"Mom? Where's Easton?" I ask.

"Shh," she says. "It's okay. He got into a fight with Jared, who knocked him out, but he's been treated, and he'll be just fine."

I heave a sigh of relief.

"I was so scared," my mother says. "I never should have left you alone. Never."

I squeeze her hand. "It's not your fault."

My father drifts in through the doorway as though he's unsure if I really want to see him, but I really do. Now that I know the truth, I know that he has to be hurting. After what Julia—or Renee—did to him, there is no going back. She tried to kill his daughter. She's a psychotic bitch. The only thing I wonder about is her baby. Is it really Dad's, or is it her boyfriend's? The whole thing is so confusing, but I'm sure they'll unravel it in court.

"Hey," my dad says, taking a seat on the opposite side of my bed. He and my mom look at each other across my piles of blankets, and they smile tentatively. It sends waves of nostalgia through me—them, tucking me into bed at night, singing silly songs and sharing stories. The books my mother brought home from the library, the lullabies my father would sing.

I must be high, because I think there might be some chance for them to get back together. But of course, that is impossible. Too much has happened. They've grown in different directions, like two branches of the same tree. And I'm the trunk. I must be delirious and full of drugs.

Starting to float away again, I feel safe and cherished.

And isn't that all anyone ever wants?

CHAPTER

73

Amelia

Newton Correctional Facility, 2021

When *Beyond the Glass* was published, I visited Gerald Shapiro. It was Christmas. I carried the present with me, which the guards checked carefully at security. I had wrapped it in a silver foil paper, with lacy red ribbons to boot. I wasn't sure what he'd think about his gift, but I was curious about his reaction, after all my hard work.

He wasn't allowed with the general population, who got the privilege of sitting with their guests in relative comfort, in a room with maroon walls and a television with *The Price Is Right* perpetually on. No, I had to meet with him in the interrogation room, and his hands were chained behind him. I had to open the present for him.

When I showed him the cover with the old computer and the title printed on the screen, he chuckled and said, "What's *Beyond the Glass*?"

"A monster," I whispered.

"Well, you got that part right," he said.

"I didn't know if you wanted me to sign it . . ." I said, half joking.

He surprised me by exclaiming, "Of course I do!"

So I signed it with my usual note—*You never know who's on the other side.* I wasn't sure if he got it, but he thanked me, nevertheless.

I looked around the room, and then my eyes rested on the one-way mirror. We were being observed, of course. That was the way Gerald has lived half his life. I wondered if he felt like a tiger in a zoo. He didn't seem to mind it. He'd always been forthcoming with me.

"Why did you open up to me?" I ask, genuinely interested in the answer.

He cocks his head thoughtfully.

"The way you talked to me . . . It made me wonder why I do what I do. And if I can change."

"Do you think that's possible?"

I thought about all the research I'd done on him and serial killers over the years. Did he have the capacity to change? Did he have anything to contribute to the world, or should he just be put to death? I wasn't sure of the answer. Maybe I never would be.

CHAPTER 74

Gabby

Iowa City, 2025

THE BELL RINGS, and I grab my backpack and sling it over my shoulder. Everyone is in a rush to get out the door, out into the sunshine, in the world away from here. I walk past my father's classroom, but on second thought, I duck my head inside the door. He is wiping off the white board, some notes about iambic pentameter.

"How was your day?" I ask, sitting on a desk.

He looks terrible, with wrinkled clothes and rumpled hair, bloodshot eyes and a five o'clock shadow. He should have taken more time off. Me, I was out of school for a couple of weeks before I felt up to coming back.

"Another day in paradise," he says. It's how he always answers that question, but I know he's not feeling it. He flashes me a sad smile.

"Do you want to have a picnic this weekend?" I ask.

It's something we did when I was little. We'd get fried chicken and then head to the lake and sit on a towel on the beach, throwing biscuits to the ducks and laughing.

"Sounds like a plan," he says.

I dangle my foot, trying to think of the way I want to word my question.

"Do you miss her?"

He knows who I'm talking about.

Julia. Who else?

He must feel so betrayed—that she would try to hurt me, that she tried to implicate him in Bridget's kidnapping. I found out she told the police that he had pictures of Bridget on his phone, but she was lying, of course. And she was the one who left that note at my house, about me being next. She'd used his key to get in.

She was arrested for conspiracy to commit murder. Her trial will be in a few months. Those things move way more slowly than I ever thought. I'm relieved to know that she's behind bars and can't mess with my dad's head anymore. It's weird, she was the one who was so young, but she definitely wore the pants in that relationship.

She refused to take a paternity test to determine whether the baby belonged to Jared or my father. My dad's open to taking care of the baby, given that Jared is out of the picture, but Julia wants the baby to go to her mom. As long as the baby has someone other than her. She proved herself to be quite psycho.

"I don't miss her," he says. "Well, I guess I miss who she used to be, or who I thought she was. I know you never liked her, but she was really a bright girl, full of ideas and excitement. It just got away from her, though. She was obsessed with her father."

"I'm sure she cared about you," I say, but I'm not certain it's true.

He takes a deep breath and goes to his desk, organizing his papers. "Doesn't matter."

"Well . . . I guess I'll see you tomorrow," I say, wishing that I didn't have to leave him alone. But we'll see each other over the weekend. He'll be fine.

We'll both be fine.

I walk to the parking lot, and I see Easton sitting in the driver's seat of his clunker of a car, waiting for me. Grinning, I slide into the passenger seat and lean over to kiss him. We've hardly been apart since that night. He picks me up in the morning, comes to my house after school (since my mom isn't really letting me go anywhere at the moment), and leaves late at night. We do our homework together, watch endless movies, and basically just enjoy being alive, together.

As we're pulling out, we see Bridget walking on the grass. She's alone.

"Hold on," I say, and Easton pulls off to the side. "Let's see if she wants to come over."

He nods, and I roll down the window and call to her.

"Bridget! You wanna come hang out?"

She turns to look at me, and for a moment I see apprehension cross her face. I recognize it as an expression that I've caught on my face a few times since our ordeal. But then it melts away, giving way to a smile.

She tucks a strand of hair behind her ear. "I'd like that."

I pull my seat forward so she can crawl into the back seat.

When she's settled, Easton puts the car back into gear, and we head toward my house.

It's wrong what they say, about three being a crowd.

To me, these days, it's safety in numbers.

And who couldn't use more friends?

CHAPTER 75

Amelia

Iowa City, 2025

Although it is March, the cemetery is still covered with light patches of snow. This is spring in the Midwest. I am flanked by my daughter on one side and my father on the other. Isaac is waiting in the car. Tragedy has brought us together yet again. It seems to have thawed the pain of my mother's death, and it's almost like we are burying my mother all over again.

Her tombstone is simple. A marble headstone. Her name. The date of her birth, the date of her death. A little clay statue that Gabby left on the ledge of the stone when she was still in elementary school.

I don't come here much anymore, especially since *Beyond the Glass* was published. There was a layer of guilt that coated me back in those days, when my father was so angry that I wrote about her story in a book all about a serial killer. But I don't think my mother would have minded. In fact, I think she'd have been proud of me.

I don't bring flowers here, because that's what Gerald was carrying to his supposed wife's grave, when he tricked my mother so he could take advantage of her and kill her. That's why I brought my daughter, so she could know my mother even though she never met her.

I like to picture my mom somewhere, watching us carry on her memory.

I look at my mother's name and I imagine it among the names of all of Gerald's victims. They could fill a cemetery, the girls he stole away from this world. Her story, as theirs, will live on through the thousands of readers who read *Beyond the Glass*.

The companion book, which is set to be released late next year, explores a much more uplifting story—the one of the survivors. There are more than I realized, and they came out of the woodwork after Bridget's kidnapping. I interviewed them, asking about their dreams and accomplishments, the hope that can come after the storm.

These are the stories that matter.

It's true that some people can never get enough of serial killers. Of violence. And I know that it's because it's been almost celebrated in pop culture. It's fascinating, the chaos they create through their terrible work. Maybe not, though, if we really think about it. Guys chasing girls with butcher knives. I'd rather look at what's behind the horrific impulse to want to destroy someone, the thirst for power.

But the truth is that destruction isn't power. Creation is.

ACKNOWLEDGMENTS

There are so many people who made this book possible.

First of all, I want to thank Katie Monson at SBR Media, who took a chance on me and believed in my book. Her reassurance and guidance were integral as we moved through the submission process. I'd also like to thank Terri Bischoff, who saw promise in my book and offered me the chance to make my dreams come true.

Thomas Wickersham has been a pleasure to work with, and all his suggestions made my book that much stronger. I'd also like to mention the rest of the team at Crooked Lane Books: Thairsheemarie Fantauzzi Perez, Julia Abbott, Rebecca Nelson, Stephanie Manova, Megan Matti, Melissa Rechter, and Monica Manzo. Debbie Stone was also crucial in ridding my book of those pesky grammatical mistakes.

My beta reader, Blu McCormick, deserves a special shout-out. Her encouragement kept me going and helped shape the book into what it ultimately became.

I'm so grateful to Lisa Renee-Jones Harrison and Christina Henry for reading and commenting on my book. So kind of you.

Thanks as well to my family, who supported me throughout the process: my husband, Shane; my daughter, Evie; and my son, Finn.